Dagger of Destiny

DoD, Volume 1

Victor Frederijk

Published by Victor Frederijk, 2024.

DAGGER OF DESTINY

First edition. July 29, 2024.

Copyright © 2024 Victor Frederijk.

ISBN: 979-8227939036

Written by Victor Frederijk.

Table of Contents

Chapter 1

It was very early in the morning.

Four in the morning to be more precise. Vani's eyes were burning from the bright lights and lack of sleep. He could almost feel the redness in his sleep-deprived eyes. His tolerance for everything around him was low, and he relied on the chemical boosts given to him through coffee and cigarettes to keep him going. He was at the one place he disliked more than a hospital, the airport. The company he worked for had a business opportunity in Mozambique to supply a large mine with condition-monitoring equipment for their fleet of mining vehicles. Vani and Jacob had been tasked to visit the customer in Mozambique's northern region, in the Moatize province.

The flight left from OR Tambo airport in Johannesburg and required them to be at the airport three hours ahead of the flight time. Three hours! Vani was cursing in his mind, *why on earth did we need to be there so early*? Nothing of this sat well with him, not the lack of sleep, nor his digestive system which was not happy with coffee so early in the morning. Getting up so early meant he'd had to miss his morning training session – keeping his well-muscled, 80kg frame fit and strong was a priority. *And I'll also miss my MMA session tonight*, he thought grumpily.

As he moved through the airport, he noticed how everyone there was being moved like sheep through the narrow lines and gates. For a second, he wondered if this was all that life had to offer. Did studying for 10 years after school mean being subjected to this form of passive-aggressive torture?

Vani never really enjoyed travelling for work as it required a lot of preparation. He liked to plan in advance and prepare accordingly. His packing method was somewhat painful in that he always packed according to the 'What if?' question.

What if I get a migraine? I better pack meds for that.

What if I get a stomach bug? Let me put in some Imodium.

What if there isn't toilet paper? I better pack a roll.

What if the shower is dirty? I'll take flip-flops and disinfectant.

What if I get hungry during the night? I'll pack some energy bars just in case.

And so on...

After passing through airport security, he made his way to the business lounge. *Last chance to eat something decent before the flight,* he thought. *Also, the last chance to make use of clean toilet facilities.* In the lounge, he met up with his senior colleague Jacob. They were glad to see each other and exchanged their experiences of what a disruption such an early flight was. Jacob admitted that the only benefit was the reduced amount of traffic on the roads so early in the morning. Vani checked his phone. *Nothing yet from Saskia, she must still be sleeping,* he thought. *I'll just send her a message once we're on the plane.* Saskia was his sweetheart and had been his first love in high school. They had drifted apart after university, but Saskia had reestablished contact after Vani's divorce.

It was time to board their flight, and Vani lifted his suitcase into the overhead compartment with ease and settled down. From time to time, he glanced at his phone with the photo of his children as his wallpaper; he hoped they were still sleeping well. His six-year-old twins, Astrid and Kate, were the love of his life. The divorce had been rough, although as responsible parents they had tried their best to shelter the children from the arguments. Vani's divorce had left him with a coldness of heart which he did not like. He wanted to get stronger and feel less hurt by the process, however, he got it wrong, and instead of getting stronger, he just got colder and more suspicious of people.

ON THE PLANE, HE AND Jacob had seats close to the front of the plane, which made boarding a bit more pleasant. It also meant that storage space in the overhead compartment wasn't an issue. This thought was triggered when Vani noticed how many people were breaking the 'rules' of what carry-on luggage should be. One or two small suitcases, not half your house as some people were doing. During the flight, when the air hostess started to serve breakfast, Vani thought that he should perhaps try out the airplane food, as it might be his absolute last chance to eat something decent. The food and preparation thereof in any African country left much to be desired on these business trips. The food on the plane was plain, flavourless, and stale. Although he didn't know it then, it was better than what would be waiting for him.

AS THE PLANE TOUCHED down at Moatize airport, the captain gave the usual farewell and comment on the outside temperature, but Vani s wasn't paying attention. As the passengers shuffled to the front of the plane in preparation to depart, the air hostess waited for the stairs before opening the door. This was the last experience of comfort he would have for a long time. When the plane's door opened, the heat punched his whole being and it felt like he was being shoved into a furnace. The area was experiencing a heatwave and it was 47 degrees Celsius at 09:00 in the morning.

Vani switched his phone off airplane mode, but to his surprise, he had no cellphone reception. 'That useless accountant that manages our phone contracts didn't activate our international roaming, for fuck's sake,' Vani said in frustration to Jacob as they walked down the airplane stairs. 'Our only connection now will be the Wi-Fi at the hotel,' Jacob replied calmly. Perhaps because he was happy to have some peace and quiet from his wife of 40 years.

The security at the airport was strict with a strong military presence. Military personnel escorted everyone through customs and prevented pictures from being taken. Vani found this kind of amusing, as the airport was a run-down building that looked like an old Victorian farmhouse.

A brief moment of unease came over Vani as he recalled the threat level and the news headlines about a terrorist group moving around and growing in the northern parts of Mozambique. Before their trip, Vani had completed an online corporate travel request, which gave an indication of threat levels for destination countries. The identified threat level for Mozambique had been 'moderate,' which was the same for South Africa, so Vani had not paid much attention. But now he wasn't feeling quite so relaxed.

On their way through customs, Vani asked Jacob, 'Do you think they have the guards here because of the terrorist threat that has been going on?'

'From what I read, the threat was way more north than where we are going, so maybe it's just a precautionary measure,' Jacob replied.

After passing through customs, they met a local driver assigned by their travel agent. He was a very friendly character named Angry. Irony was lost on the local population it seemed. They loaded their luggage and set off to the hotel they were staying at. The scenery on the way left much to be desired. To be blunt, it was an eyesore. Groups of people wandered and loitered along the roadside, occasionally waving down one of the many small motorcycles that functioned as the local taxi service. The roads were in dire condition, and the streets and neighbourhoods were riddled with trash. There was a grimy feel to the whole place. It seemed the only structured institutions were the mining operations, whilst the rest lived up to the general expectations of a degraded African country.

They reached their hotel, which was next to a main road. It appeared half decent from the outside. After checking in they took their bags to their respective rooms. Vani opened the door, and was amazed to see an air conditioner in the room. That was where the happiness ended for him. The floor was covered in fine black dust, no doubt from the big trucks hauling coal through the main road. He switched his air conditioner on, and then left to go to the meeting scheduled with their distributor. On the way, Vani quickly took a detour through the dining room to gauge the level of food he could expect. It didn't look promising.

THE MEETING TOOK PLACE on the premises of BBB Enterprises in Tete. The owner, Benjamin, was a bit of an oddball; it looked like he should have been cast in a role in a surfer movie next to Matthew McConaughey. He looked out of place; however, this was Africa, and doing business here meant dealing with all types of characters.

There was a lengthy discussion on the opportunity of getting business from one of the large coal mines in the area. The meeting ended on a positive note, and Benjamin was excited to get support from Vani and Jacob.

They headed out for lunch at a restaurant on the Zambezi River. The temperature was now sitting at 50 degrees Celsius. After ordering a few beers Benjamin remarked, 'You guys have picked the warmest time ever to come here.'

'So, this is extreme for you as well?' Vani asked.

'Yes, this is hectic,' Benjamin replied, 'and the beers won't even cool us down, we could never get drunk on beer in this temperature. We would just sweat the alcohol out.'

'Where does your company come from, is there a meaning behind the triple Bs?' Jacob asked Benjamin.

'Of course, but I can't go around telling everyone the true meaning...' Benjamin leaned closer to Jacob and whispered, 'It stands for Bullshit Baffles Brains.'

They both burst out laughing and raised their beers to cheers to Benjamin's odd but funny explanation. After that, they enjoyed a quiet and relaxing lunch on the Zambezi River bank. Vani was amazed to see so much water flowing in one place; it was the biggest river he had ever seen. 'So Vani, we've spoken a lot over the phone and email, but this is the first time we are meeting face to face. What is your background in the industry, tell me a bit more about yourself,' Benjamin asked.

'Well, that is not an easy question to answer, haha,' Vani replied. But Benjamin didn't drop his gaze and obviously expected a more decent and complete answer. Vani noticed this immediately and continued, 'After completing my mechanical engineering degree, I did my practical work in a steel mill. From there I tried to move around as much as possible to gain experience in different industries, so I worked for about two years at one place at a time and then moved on. Before my current company I worked at a place that manufactures explosives for the mining industry, where I completed my explosive engineering training. And now for the last five years, I've been with this company in the technical sales role.'

Benjamin paid close attention to what Vani was saying, showing a true interest in Vani's history. 'Wow, explosives? That sounds interesting,' he replied.

'Not really, it was for mining applications, so no destruction or demolition fun stuff,' Vani responded.

After lunch, Vani and Jacob returned to their hotel for the night. In the parking lot, they planned the agenda and pick-up time for the next day, and waved goodbye to Benjamin as he drove off to his home. Vani and Jacob agreed to meet at the hotel bar for a few nightcaps before retiring. Upon returning to his room, Vani was grateful that he'd switched the air conditioner on before leaving as the room was a bit cooler than the outside temperature, though not as cold as he had hoped for. The small air con was struggling to keep up with the heatwave.

THE SUN CAME UP EARLY the next morning and the heat had barely dropped during the night. It was going to be another scorcher of a day. Vani walked down to the dining hall for the breakfast buffet, and not to his surprise, the food looked horrible. The coffee tasted like it was mixed in with some soil, and even the sugar seemed artificial and unrefined. Looking at the options at the buffet, Vani tried to pick food that would be the least likely to cause an upset stomach. *Polony! Who in their right mind would substitute bacon with polony and still think it is acceptable*? Vani wondered. There was no way he was going to eat processed meat from a Third World country with no quality control processes in place. It appeared that fried eggs and toast would be the safest option for his digestive tract.

Breakfast was done, and Benjamin was due to pick them up for their visit to the mining site. Before leaving, Vani brushed his teeth again, trying ridiculously hard not to swallow any of the tap water. It was always a struggle visiting countries where the tap water wasn't drinkable, and showering with your mouth closed the whole time. It was a lot harder than a person would think.

Whilst travelling to the site, conversation touched on the hot weather again, and how in the mining pit it could be another 20 degrees Celsius hotter. The scenery on the way to the site remained just as dismal as it had been the previous day. Once they exited Moatize it started to look more like bushveld and felt a bit more homely.

At the site entrance, they found heavy security and slow reactions. With their patience being tried and tested and their corporate clothes becoming sweat-soaked, they eventually got onto the site and met with some of the engineers to discuss solutions and product offerings. The various meetings were all positive; end users were grateful to see guests travel so far for them.

It was past midday, and the time had flown by quickly with all the meetings and moving around on site. As they made their way back to their vehicle, Vani's stomach gave an audible growl. 'Gents, I'm really hungry now, my small breakfast didn't last me long, in fact, I'm so hungry now I could eat the arse off a low-flying duck.' This caused a bit of a chuckle and they agreed to go for lunch on the Zambezi River bank again.

As they neared the carpark, a series of bangs and shots could be heard in the distance. 'Sounds like they are blasting in the mining pit,' Jacob said.

In the far distance, they could see people running. Mine workers dispersing in all different directions. It sounded like the bushveld was on fire with the non-stop crackling noises. 'Does that sound like gunfire to you?' Vani asked. 'Maybe a flammable store caught fire or something?'

Then like a tidal wave, the three businessmen saw hundreds of men in camo running towards the mining site, firing guns and brandishing machetes. They came down a hill close to the entrance of the mine, charging like it was a race. It looked like an army of termites had got wind of food and every termite was storming out of the nest to get to the food source. Most of them were armed with AK47 automatic rifles, others with machetes, and a few with RPG rocket launchers. They were loud, filled with malice, firing shots, and clearly taking no prisoners. 'Fuck! That must be the Islamic terrorist group!' shouted Jacob. 'Run!'

He was right. It was the group known as ISIS-M; an African branch of the group globally known as ISIS. These local militants belonging to an Islamic terrorist group had targeted the mining site. They wanted to seize it, planning to control the wealth it brought to the local region.

Chapter 2

The three businessmen stood in complete and utter disbelief. They looked at the spectacle trying to figure out how this was even possible. Only when the militants got closer and a stray bullet hit the car standing next to them, did it sink in. This was real. They were caught completely off guard and unprepared. Even Vani's extensive packing preparation would never cover something like this. They were caught in a terrorist attack.

The terrorists had no clear uniform, although there was a consistent theme to their attire; green camouflage pants and jackets with worn-out T-shirts that looked like they had been picked up off the floor. They'd covered their faces with various cloths, with camouflage and black looking to be like the trending fashion statement for their cause. Their headwear prevented them from being individually identified and only their eyes were exposed. Red bloodshot eyes with dilated pupils. Eyes filled with unreasonable blind malice and hatred. Their swift actions echoed that malignant intent; they were shooting, hacking, and beating people to death without rhyme or reason.

As the bullet ricocheted off the car, their fight or flight response kicked in. 'Get down!' shouted Jacob. As Vani dropped to the dirt, he found his mouth dry and his throat choked up. However, he was far from choking; his shallow and rapid breathing meant his oesophagus was expanding to allow for more oxygen as his mind was preparing his body to take action.

Whilst down on their hands and knees, the three men looked around desperately, trying to figure out a possible path they could take to escape. They were unarmed and outnumbered, there was no way fighting would lead to survival. They started weaving through cars, moving away from the oncoming threat, and making their way back into the mining site. In a low voice, Vani asked Benjamin, 'You know this site better than us, is there anywhere we can go to get out of here?!'

'We could try and make for the heavy vehicle workshop and from there make a run for the mine's south-eastern gate, but...' Benjamin paused.

'But what?!' Jacob asked frantically.

'But that takes us further away from the road that leads us back to Moatize. It leads us into the bushveld area with hills and difficult terrain. Nothing about that trip on foot is something we are capable of.' Benjamin replied anxiously as he considered their options.

'We need to get out of here, and if it is the bad option, so be it! A bad plan now is better than a good plan tomorrow!' Vani exclaimed impatiently. Benjamin seemed to be in a state of shock that had paralysed him, and Jacob gave him a shove. 'Listen here, boet, we need to move *now*! So, we all keep low and start heading in the direction of the south-eastern gate. Get your ass into gear and lead the way!'

Benjamin took the lead, and they all kept as low as they could whilst doing short sprints from tree to tree and between covering positions. Vani slung his laptop bag onto his back and tightened the straps as they were moving. They continued to peer anxiously over their shoulders to determine the terrorists' movements. So far, the danger appeared to be approaching faster than they were able to get away. 'Let's pick up the pace a bit,' Vani said to Benjamin, 'at this rate, they are going to catch up to us.'

Benjamin moved faster and soon they entered the heavy vehicle machine workshop. They began weaving in between large mining dump trucks and making their way to the exit at the opposite end. An earlier tour before their site meeting with the workshop supervisor through the vehicle service area helped them navigate the area quickly. The workshop staff were running in different directions, it was chaotic, and some were even climbing into the dump trucks to hide. Arriving at the other end of the workshop, the trio exited through a service door. From here they could see the narrow path that would get them to the south-eastern gate.

The path sloped steadily downhill from the workshop to the gate and it was untouched by the chaos behind them. To their dismay, there was no cover or anywhere they could hide along the way. Beyond a few rocks and patches of dry grass, it was a barren piece of land. Their anxiety built up as they eyed the daunting one-kilometre stretch that lay ahead of them. Beyond the gate and boundary fence, there was a maintained bushveld line with trees and grass coverage. That met the foot of a low mountain range with bushy and rocky terrain. The trees looked inviting, offering them security and shelter from the threat behind them. 'If we can make it to the bush then we should be able to hide for now,' Benjamin said.

'If we are to run for it, there is no looking back, don't hesitate,' Vani said. 'And Jacob, as the oldest, you should lead so we don't outpace you. Move as fast as you can, we'll keep up with you and stay together as a group.' Jacob nodded, not arguing with Vani's reasoning nor taking offence to the statement.

Jacob took the first step and soon picked up the pace to a light jog. They kept close to each other, staying on his heels. The sweat poured from them under the hot African sun. The heatwave was still going strong and made this stretch feel like an oven. Halfway to the gate, Jacob noticed movement ahead.

'Can you make out what is moving up ahead? Is it still safe?' he asked.

'Not sure,' Vani replied, trying to wipe away the constant flow of sweat into his eyes, causing them to burn and blur his vision. 'Benjamin, can you make out what is going on?'

'Let's get closer and then try and figure it out,' Benjamin replied.

They kept on jogging until they were close to the gate, then Jacob slowed the pace and they looked around anxiously. There was no movement or anyone in sight. They scanned around for the security guard from the mine who should be safeguarding this point of exit, but there was no one.

Breathing heavily, they cautiously proceeded to the palisade gate and opened it. Whilst making their way out, a low whistle came from the bush in front of them. Shocked, their eyes darted into the shrubbery, but they could not see anything. Suddenly a hand appeared from behind a tree, waving at them, trying to get their attention. The trio stood frozen solid, not sure if it was a threat or an invitation. No one said a word, as they looked desperately at each other for answers with panic in their eyes.

Slowly standing upright, a man appeared from behind the tree. It was the gate security guard that they had been searching for a few moments earlier. He had heard what was happening on his two-way radio and decided to take cover and hide in the bush.

Recognising his uniform and understanding his intention to help them, the trio dashed towards the guard to join him in his hiding spot. Everyone sat quietly on the ground, listening to the continuous gunfire in the distance. After a short while, Vani softly asked the guard, 'Can you help us get out of here?'

The trio stared with apprehension at the guard, yearning to get some positive news, looking for some glitter of hope. 'As pessoas más estão atacando o site,' the guard replied.

'Aggg no, fuck's sake, Portuguese, really?' Jacob responded.

The guard replied, 'Eu não fui treinado para essa merda.'

'Benjamin, you better understand what this guy is saying,' Vani said, 'or else we have a new headache on our hands.'

A fleeting grin appeared on Benjamin's face. 'Relax guys, he's scared and doesn't know what to do and yes, I understand him.'

Chapter 3

The four men moved into the bush close to the foot of the mountain to get slightly better coverage. They peered back towards the area of attack in dismay, overcome with fear and unsure of what to do next. The bushes provided some relief from the heat and the threat of being spotted. They watched as the militants made their way through each building and workshop, taking some mine workers as hostages, whilst others who showed any signs of resistance were shot on sight.

'I think we should wait here until nightfall before we start moving again, this whole scene is too intense and it might calm down later,' said Vani. 'Also, we should be harder to spot at night, so if we move slowly, we might be able to slip away.' Jacob and Benjamin agreed with the plan and Benjamin explained it to the guard in Portuguese. Despite this logical rationale, the guard was not fond of the idea of hanging around the mining site and wanted to get away as soon as possible. But he was outnumbered in votes and the decision was made to stay put until dusk.

Time went by very slowly; they were helpless and frightened witnessing the inhumane acts of violence in the distance. Vani sent up numerous silent prayers, asking for strength and mercy so that he could see his daughters again and not have them grow up without a father. There was no atheist in the bush that day, everyone was praying for a way out.

Dusk eventually crept in over the hills, filling the sky with red, and reflecting the blood that had been shed beneath it. Jacob's legs were cramping up from staying still for so long and possible dehydration was setting in. 'My legs are so stiff and painful, I'm going to have trouble moving,' he said.

For the first time since the attack, Vani could think a bit more clearly now that he was no longer in frantic survival mode. He opened his laptop bag and took out three bottles of water that he had taken from the board room after their site meeting. 'Here guys, have some water. We'll need to ration it so that we can share it with the guard.'

The lukewarm water revived them all slightly and Jacob seemed to ease up a bit. There weren't a lot of trees that would provide cover on the hills behind them, so they would have to move carefully. The sweltering day had transformed into a hot night, and the crew began to move up the hills. There was still a lot of activity on the mining site, but with their backs turned to the war zone, their focus was on trying to move quietly and stay low. The hills proved to be a bigger challenge for Jacob than anticipated. Vani and Benjamin stayed close to Jacob, one in front and one behind him, to help him get over rocks and up steep inclines. The guard moved with them; however, he kept his own pace and didn't assist the trio.

The group didn't speak much, apart from the occasional repetitive questions, 'Are we going in the right direction?' and, 'Do you hear anything?' The ground was hard, and the heat rose out of the earth after a day of being baked by the blazing sun. Sweat dripped off them as if they were still walking in the heat of the day.

Eventually, they made it to the highest point which provided them with a 360-degree view of the surrounding area. The group stood still for a moment and looked back for the first time at the mining site. In the distance, they could see the terrorists driving around and still firing gunshots into the air. Even with only the faint light provided by the moon, it was a dire sight. It was coupled with the muted screams of those poor souls that had been captured by the terrorists. Presumably, they were being murdered, raped, and tortured.

Hearing the desperate screams, the group's fear turned into grief. 'I once read,' said Vani softly, 'that after a war, monks from the East would go to look at the burning bodies, and by directly confronting the aftermath of violence, it strengthened their commitment to peaceful living. I agree. After what we saw today, I think I've had my fill of pain and suffering to last a lifetime.'

Jacob nudged Vani and the group turned to get moving again. They started their descent off the hilltop, leaving the gruesome sight behind them.

GOING DOWN PROVED TREACHEROUS with the limited light, and each member of the group fell a few times, losing their grip and slipping on the uneven ground and loose gravel. The guard was moving in front of them, ensuring he was far enough not to have to help them, but close enough to get the feeling of safety provided by moving in numbers. Benjamin, now a bit more at ease with the distance between them and the site, asked the guard what his name was.

'Chico,' he replied but said nothing more, making no attempt to make conversation or show interest in his fellow travellers.

'Thank you for helping us escape, Chico, are you from these parts?' Benjamin asked, trying to make some friendly chit-chat. However, Chico was not having any of it.

Finally, they reached the bottom of their descent. There was still sufficient night-time left for them to move towards the main road and make for the town of Moatize. Then misfortune struck... Vani stepped on a loose rock that gave way underneath his left foot and his ankle twisted painfully.

'Arrrggg... Ma se... Mother... Fucker!' Vani exclaimed.

'What happened?' Jacob asked anxiously, thinking it might be a snake bite.

'I twisted my ankle and it's freaking sore. I think I've sprained it, I can barely put weight on my foot,' Vani replied. 'But we have to keep moving, I'll power through it for now.'

Vani knew they had to move as far as possible whilst the darkness of night could protect them. Unfortunately, their travelling speed was now even more reduced because of Vani's injury. Chico seemed unhappy with their new pace, and started to move a little further out in front of them. Benjamin tried to help by putting Vani's arm over his shoulder to support his weight, but this caused him even more discomfort. Plus, the uneven terrain made such a gesture painful for both parties.

The remaining stretch to the main road was relatively flat with short shrubs, bushes, and grass covering the ground. There were few trees in sight. The group crouched in the limited cover considering their options.

'This is very dangerous, we have no cover, and our speed is too slow to get to the main road before dawn,' Vani said. 'Perhaps you should carry on without...' Vani hadn't finished his sentence when Jacob interrupted him.

'We all stick together, and we are getting out of here together!'

The notion of camaraderie gave Vani some comfort, as he would never have left anyone behind, but it was good to hear it echoed by someone else.

'Thanks, Jacob,' was all that Vani got out.

THE SUN'S FIRST RAYS started bending over the earth and dawn was upon them. The group was still about three to four kilometres from the main road with Chico still venturing out in front at a distance. Suddenly, Vani spotted a pickup truck racing towards them from a distance. It was then in absolute shock that they realised their path was crossing the same route that the terrorists used to invade the mine.

The trio fell to the ground immediately. 'Chico! Chico! Get down!' Benjamin shouted.

But Chico did not hear them until it was too late and was spotted by the occupants of the pickup truck. There were three terrorists in the front of the truck and six in the back, all of them armed with automatic rifles. Once they spotted him, they changed their course and headed directly for him, the engine revving high, and the lights bouncing up and down on the rough terrain. Chico ran towards the main road, but it was a futile effort as the truck caught up to him in no time. Bewildered, he threw his hands up in the air to show no threat or possession of a weapon.

When the pickup truck pulled up next to Chico, all six members jumped off the back and surrounded him, guns pointed at him threateningly. They shouted in Portuguese to keep his hands up and fall to his knees, which Chico did without hesitation. He could sense they had no tolerance for disobedience. Despite his cooperation, one of the terrorists smashed him on the head with the back end of his rifle. Blood poured over his face from the wound, shining bright as it fell onto the African dust. The terrorists laughed as he collapsed and kicked at him.

The three businessmen looked on in disbelief, this inhumanity was something they had never experienced before. Benjamin was in complete shock, his hands started shaking, his breathing became increasingly shallow, and it was clear that fear had overtaken him. In a pure panic, he scrambled to his feet and started running back the way the group had come, making himself visible to one of the six extremists. The attentive terrorist immediately started shouting, making the remainder of his gang aware of another escapee.

The group began to shoot in his direction, and the driver of the pickup truck gave chase. The bullets were flying over Vani and Jacob's heads. The two stayed low and quiet. Vani kept his eyes shut as he curled into a bundle to make himself as small as possible. Within a few seconds, the pickup truck caught up with Benjamin, and the other two occupants jumped out to capture him. The headlights were shining over him as the two shadowy figures approached with their rifles aimed directly at him.

The two terrorists commanded Benjamin to get down onto the ground. He put up no resistance, his emotional state was broken.

'Please, please don't kill me. I've got money, I will give you money if you let me go! Please!' Benjamin begged them to spare his life and to release him, but it was all in vain. The terrorists had no intention of letting anyone leave the site alive.

The driver of the pickup truck got out, leaving the engine idling, and made his way over to Benjamin who was sprawled out on the ground face down. He looked down at Benjamin with a smirk of disgust on his face. 'You devil of men, you thought you could outrun your destiny with death. No, no, no. You are mine now, you belong to me. But... if you, the devil with straight hair, show us where the rest of your friends are, then we will let you go.' Benjamin kept quiet; in his heart he knew this offer could not be trusted. Frustrated with the silence, the driver kicked Benjamin in the face. Blood poured from his broken nose, flowing down his chin, and his eyes watered from the injury. Benjamin could feel his world shrinking, there was nothing outside this tragedy.

In between the group of six terrorists with Chico, and Benjamin with his capturers, lay Jacob and Vani in a patch of grass coverage. They did not dare to move even a muscle for fear of being discovered. The driver ordered his two comrades to load the hostage onto the back of the pickup truck. Following his orders, they bound Benjamin's hands with barbed wire and shoved him onto the back of the vehicle, jumping on with him to prevent him from making any attempts to escape. The driver got into the truck, revved its engine and started making their way back to where Chico and their other comrades remained.

A few moments later, the entire hunting party was reunited, and the driver made Chico the same empty promise of letting him go if he revealed any other escapees. Benjamin overheard the offer and to his despair, Chico acknowledged that there were three white men with him, trying to escape. The driver nodded slowly with an evil grin on his face. 'Tell me more, we already have one, where are the other two?'

Chico pointed in the direction from which they had come. 'They should be behind us, somewhere in the grass coverage. One is an old man and the other has an injured foot. Please, boss, let me go now.'

The driver gave the other terrorists the order to walk in groups of three next to the vehicle to cover more area in their search for Vani and Jacob. The other two were to remain on the back of the pickup truck to guard their two hostages. The vehicle moved forward at a slow pace, with the soldiers walking next to the vehicle and their rifles pointing forward, ready to shoot anyone who tried to run. Jacob could see them coming and there was no way to escape. He stood up slowly, his hands raised in surrender. As soon as they spotted him, the terrorists started shouting and converging on his position, quickening their pace.

'Vani, you should get up, there is nowhere left for us to go,' Jacob said and with that, Vani also got up with his hands in the air.

Chapter 4

Within a matter of seconds, the terrorist soldiers surrounded Jacob and Vani. Guns pointed at them from every direction and the headlights of the pickup truck illuminating the scene. Although the sun was beginning to make its appearance, it was still eerily dusty and grey, causing the headlights to blind Vani. He could not make out who was where and exactly how many extremists surrounded them. The driver got out of the vehicle, and addressed them.

'I am the captain of our great General Koji Bemin, who has delivered us from your evil greed and Western capitalism. You will call me Captain Kgoto, for the fleeting time you are still alive. I will deliver you to our general and I receive great honour and glory as my reward.'

Chico's desperate cries were heard from the back of the pickup truck. 'Please Boss! Please Captain Kgoto! I showed you where they were hiding, please let me go now!' The captain frowned and ordered his two soldiers to bring Chico to the front of the truck. The three businessmen watched anxiously, fearing the worst. The captain walked over to the shaking and pleading guard, took a pistol out of his holster and cocked it, and uttered the last words Chico would ever hear. 'I don't need a low life like you, you mean nothing to me.' He placed his pistol between Chico's eyes and pulled the trigger. No hesitation, no remorse, no regard for life. The two soldiers that held Chico up, let him go and his lifeless body fell to the ground, creating a small dust cloud that drifted past the headlights.

Reeling in shock and sick to their stomachs at what they had just witnessed, Jacob and Vani did as they were told for fear that they would meet the same demise. As the terrorists shoved Jacob and Vani onto the back with Benjamin, not one of the three businessmen said a word. The soldiers climbed up beside them and kept their rifles pointed at their captives. The space on the back of the truck was cramped and the three men discovered the foul stench of their captors matched their barbaric actions.

The ride was bumpy, the driver did not care to avoid obstacles and had no regard for the vehicle or its occupants. The trio knew they were in a bad spot, however, when the ride ended, they would go from the frying pan into the fire. A cool breeze caressing Vani's face during the ride brought him no comfort, he could only imagine his approaching fate.

The vehicle made its way to the main entrance of the mining site which was now completely under terrorist control with Islamic banners hanging from the security building. As they drove in, they were greeted with cheers from their comrades and the soldiers on the truck fired shots of celebration into the air. The terrorists had occupied one of the office buildings as their headquarters for their operations. With it being a three-storey building, they kept the Western and foreign hostages on the first floor.

They had divided the floors according to various functions and ranks. The ground floor was mainly soldiers and ammunition supplies, which had a lot of movement through it. The first floor was for hostages and had a heavy guard presence to prevent anyone from escaping. The second floor was for the captains, stolen and looted items of value, drugs, and of course, their general. They pushed the three businessmen into a large open-plan office on the first floor which had been cleared of furniture. There were already about eighty other hostages being held captive, all foreign nationals from countries such as Brazil, Europe, the UK, the USA, China, and South Africa.

The prisoners were slumped on the floor, dirty from the day, sweaty from the heat, and bloody from the beatings. There was no food or water in sight and for a toilet, they had to use a bucket in the middle of the room. The conditions were dire and fear radiated from every one of the detainees.

It had now been about sixteen hours since the attack and the outside world was starting to get bits of information about the invasion. As the morning sun began to heat the room, the door was flung open and the general strode in to address the hostages and declare his intentions. The moment he entered, the guards who were slouched around jumped to their feet and dropped their eyes respectfully, saluting as he passed.

The general looked over the crowd of scared faces, and said, 'The world now knows we are here and that we have liberated this area. We have set up a media room on the floor above, where we will take you in small groups to show the world and use you to make our ransom demands. Some of you might live and some will die, it just depends on your value and purpose. I will see you soon to start making our broadcast and demands.'

Vani looked directly at the general, feeling nothing but disgust and anger. Sensing Vani's glare, the general walked straight up to Vani and squatted so that he could look him straight in the eyes. 'I am General Koji Bemin, I'm sure you've heard of me,' he sneered. 'Never underestimate my power.'

His bloodshot eyes peered at Vani, sweat dripping off his forehead. Vani did not know he was in the presence of a celebrity; though the general was more infamous than famous as he was sought by many government agencies. The general was on the top ten Most Wanted list, wanted by the CIA, Interpol, and the ICC for various gruesome human rights violations. He was in fact number one on the CIA's list.

Vani noticed his dirty boots, militia outfit, gold-plated pistol, and yellow bandana, but what struck him most was a dagger hanging around his neck. It looked ancient, like an old artefact and it had a green glow to it. And for a moment it felt like the dagger was drawing

Vani closer to it, offering him something, that in his mind he could not understand, but in his heart felt like an offering of salvation.

Chapter 5

The instrument of fear around the rebel leader's neck had an unworldly birthplace. The dagger was created with the hope of deliverance and freedom from evil, in complete contrast to its present use. Since the general had acquired the dagger, he had used it as a display of his power, to instil fear into those who crossed his path.

THERE EXISTED A PLANET in a different galaxy to ours, so far away that the distance in light years seemed unreal. The planet's name was Helderwoud. The planet was lush and green with an abundance of plant life,, filled with mesmerising flowers that grew in all imaginable colours and shapes. There was an abundance of fruit trees that made up forests as wide as a continent and fed an entire ecosystem beneath them. The waters on the planet were a bright luminescent blue colour and flourished with strange aquatic creatures. Due to the planet's relative distance to its bright star, it had a tropical climate and was host to many different life forms that lived in equilibrium on their planet.

One of these life forms was a small, timid and intelligent primate species, whose physical characteristics resembled a Galago or Bush Baby as it is known in South Africa. They were called the Nagapie. They would not be at the top of the food chain based on their physical attributes, for they were of small stature. However, their intellectual capabilities placed these small creatures as the most intelligent on their planet.

The Nagapie had bushy tails and human-like torsos, with large heads that housed two big yellow eyes. The tallest of them was about 10cm, and they weighed about 100g on average due to their hollow bone structure. Their fingers were quite long relative to their hands, which aided them in their tasks and way of life. The Nagapie had a love for science, research and development, and a passion for learning and developing new technologies. Their biological structure suited them very well in allowing them to create innovative technology and advancements on a nanoscale. With their small hands, they could easily create something with incredible accuracy. The Nagapie also made great strides in telepathy; however, it was almost used as a second language to transfer data more efficiently. When speaking to acquaintances or loved ones, they used their native language, which had a lot of clicking sounds in it. Data transfer was vital to them, as complex research required sharing vast amounts of data with each other.

To avoid falling prey to the predatory creatures on their planet, the Nagapie constructed a giant floating fortress called VanBo. This giant fortress had a wide and thick base with several skyscrapers on top of it. Levitation of the structure was achieved by anti-gravitational field generators that they designed and constructed themselves. Their fortress was a bustling city for the Nagapie, and it expanded each year to accommodate the newborn Nagapies and requirements for research facilities. During the night-time, several hundreds of cables would descend from the fortress and connect to the treetops of the forest below them to allow the Nagapies to gather food. Their diet consisted of bugs, fruit, nuts, and various type of seeds.

They were very intellectual as a species. In comparison to humans, they were about 800 to 1000 years more advanced in many areas. A complex social structure governed their everyday life, and they were led by a Chieftain. The title of Chieftain went to the Nagapie who was the oldest among them. Younglings would be in the constant care of their parents, accompanying them to work, and in doing so, they learnt from an incredibly young age. This meant that each generation built on the ideas and technology of the previous generation. The Chieftain's grandson was named Trix, he was well known for the advancements he had made in the field of wormholes and space travel.

What set Trix apart from the rest of the Nagapie was that he was the first to be born with blue eyes, most likely a genetic mutation carried over from his father's side. Trix was in his young adulthood, and he had been planning to start a family soon with a female who shared the same laboratory and field of study as him. Her name was Hilee. The two of them had grown up together because their mothers were colleagues as well. Hilee would often find herself lost in thought as she stared into Trix's big blue eyes. She was smitten with him, and he loved her dearly.

At the end of each working day, Trix would join the foraging teams responsible for gathering fresh insects and fruit for each night's supper. He was not obligated to join them, but he loved the wild smells of the forest and seeing the nightlife coming out. He also used this opportunity to look for the fattest and juiciest insects he could find, which were given as a token of affection to Hilee. The Nagapies ate with their respective families at night, and Hilee's family was always grinning and winking at Hilee when Trix brought them their food with Hilee's special delivery. Though the Nagapies did not have the concept of marriage, they did mate for life. So, the first partner they mated with became their lifetime companion. Consequently, they gave a great deal of consideration before making a commitment to each other with their bodies. Hilee had known for many years that her heart belonged to Trix, and should he wish it, she would become his life partner. At times she found the fact that they hadn't mated yet a bit frustrating and was hoping Trix would ask her during the coming festival.

Once a year the city of VanBo celebrated what was known as the Gift of Life with a festival that lasted three days. During the festival, the Nagapie would reflect and celebrate their existence and that of the world around them. The time had come again for their annual celebration, this year would mark the 75th festival since its implementation. For some, it was an opportunity to put their chemical skills to the test and create sweet fruity beer, for others it was an opportunity to declare their commitment to a life partner. The latter was evident four months after the festival when the city would see a giant spike in population growth.

On the first night of the festival, Trix asked Hilee to accompany him to the rooftop of their laboratory under the false pretence that they were needed for work. He had set up the area to create a romantic location and there he asked her to be his life partner. Hilee was ecstatic that the day had finally come, she leaped forward and embraced Trix shedding a tear of joy, feeling whole and fulfilled. The couple stayed on the rooftop for the remainder of the night. The following morning they announced the big news to their families and the Chieftain, and it was received with great excitement and more reason to celebrate the festival.

Trix's forefathers were the developers of their unique and powerful energy source. An energy source that was created by a fusion process of an elemental material that was only to be found on Helderwoud. They managed to create a nuclear fusion energy source that was stable, clean, and safe. The Nagapie later found that their energy source could be harnessed into a direct energy weapon that would cause great destruction on a planetary scale. And because they had always been a peaceful and passive society, the further enhancements of the energy source were halted, and the research team was moved into other areas of energy applications. And so it became that their energy powered their entire civilisation, from their homes to their transportation to the running of their planet.

Their love for science and discovery was matched only by their desire for harmony. They had built their developments around living in balance with their planet, seeking peace and improvement. Isolated in their galaxy, they were able to thrive and coexist in peace with their natural habitat. It was a utopia, untouched by the chaos and destruction that plagued other civilisations. Their research and technology had no adverse side effects or negative impacts on the planet.

However, their peaceful existence had been compromised when they created their energy source. They had not anticipated that a malicious and dark creature would seek out their discovery for its evil ambitions. This energy source emitted a specific frequency that had caught the attention of a powerful being who was responsible for the destruction of many worlds. The creature became aware of their energy source during the 70th Festival of Life celebrations, while it was invading the planet Kreub in the neighbouring galaxy to the Nagapie. The creature sought to grow more powerful by incorporating the Nagapie's energy into its own being. And by doing so, grasp the opportunity to expand its influence and control in the galaxy.

SIX MONTHS AFTER THE Festival of Life, something started to stir in the Nagapie solar system. Their department for studying planetary movement and asteroid tracking detected an object entering their solar system. The Nagapie in the lab ran through tons of data sets and calculations to conclude that the object had an unnatural velocity and the ability to avoid space debris.

An emergency council meeting was called by the head of the department, and their findings were presented to the Chieftain and a council of elders. They all agreed unanimously that the object had plotted a course that was aimed directly at Helderwoud. Based on the current speed, they had little more than a week before the object would reach them. The next question on their minds was whether this was a friend or foe. In their existence, they had never tried to make contact with life outside of Helderwoud's serenity. There were a few elders amongst them who believed it was an intelligent race seeking them out to trade technologies. However, this sounded highly unlikely to the Chieftain and the rest of the council members.

Due to their passive lifestyle, they had no means to repel an enemy from space. The weaponry was limited to staffs that shot electrical frequencies and lights to repel the large predators on their planet. The Chieftain gave the order to hold a mass meditation session with all the city's inhabitants. Mass meditation sessions were done in extremely rare circumstances, and required all the able-minded Nagapie to engage in a collective mode of telepathy. With all their minds linked up in collective telepathy, it turned their race into a living supercomputer with instantaneous communication.

The Chieftain presented the information about an object approaching them with unknown intent. At first, the collective telepathy was noisy and incoherent as the Nagapies were all shocked by the news and were trying to make sense of it. It was comparable to an online meeting with thousands of participants unmuted and speaking at the same time. The Chieftain called for everyone to calm their minds and focus on the problem at hand. As the Nagapie had no significant means of defence, the collective mind decided it would be best to safeguard their research and technology that could be used to cause harm. So, they deleted and destroyed all physical traces of anything deemed dangerous, including the historical research on their energy source. The data and research would be safe and live on as long as the Nagapie emerged unscathed from their uninvited visitors.

The food gathering teams were tasked with collecting more food each night to stockpile a supply. They searched and stored as many non-perishable foods as they could find. Trix and Hilee cleared their laboratory of potentially threatening data, which was difficult for Hilee. She took a lot of pride in her work and had recently been making breakthroughs in teleportation. Trix tried to comfort Hilee as best he could, but her hopes and dreams were shattered. Not only was her life's work gone, but she also still hadn't fallen pregnant with a youngling as they had hoped.

Chapter 6

A WEEK LATER, THE APPROACHING object passed Helderwoud's neighbouring planet, giving the Nagapie their first clear images. It was a fleet of six spacecraft. Not exploratory or supply crafts, but rather large, menacing battle cruisers flying close to each other. They had an egg-like shape with a smooth exterior. Underneath each of the battle cruisers' skin was a vast array of weaponry and tracking sensors. The cruisers had one purpose – to search and destroy.

The weapons on board each cruiser could leave a world in pain and ashes, and yet their destructive power was dwarfed by the dark power of the fleet owner. After conducting their scans and studies of the cruiser, the Nagapies knew the precautionary measurements they had taken were right, but it was not enough to ensure their survival. As the battle cruisers got closer and closer, panic and fear began to overtake the once-peaceful society. The inhabitants of Helderwoud had no idea of the danger that lurked within the shadows of the cruisers, and that their society was about to face an extinction-level threat. Death's ambassador had come for them.

The evil being known as AnaTi was a prevailing interstellar conqueror. He and his family were the only survivors of his race. Their race had originally come from a hot and barren planet with extreme desert and volcanic conditions. The planet known as Pofadder gave birth to their race, but very few beings knew of this planet's tragic history.

The appearance of the Pofadder race would stir a sober person's stomach. They were lizard-like creatures that moved around like humans on their back legs. Their skin was scaly and slimy, they had snake-like heads, and their tails were covered with spikes. The Pofadder race had many skills and powers, but one which set them apart from most living creatures was their ability to harness and create direct energy attacks. They could concentrate energy into the palms of their hands and release it in a direct energy attack that could destroy a planet. This dark and violent race had nearly destroyed themselves trying to establish more control and power over each other.

AnaTi's family consisted of his sister, JolJan, his brother TiTi, and their mother LinHo. Their relationship was a toxic blend of sibling rivalry, jealousy, and verbal sniping. Their tolerance for each other was so low that would often get into physical confrontations. Confrontations that would leave massive amounts of collateral damage in their wake. Though the siblings couldn't bear each other, they understood all too well that for them to grow their reign in the galaxy, they would need to rely on each other. Driven by an unquenchable thirst for more power, the remaining family members set out in different directions into the galaxy to grow their reign and authority.

AnaTi monitored and studied the Nagapie in the planet's orbit with his fleet of spaceships that were operated by a variety of alien species, all of whom had been captured when their worlds had been conquered by AnaTi. From the ground, the fleet of ships had now become visible with the naked eye. He looked down on the Nagapie's world with great envy of their energy source and their intellect. They could prove to be a valuable asset in his arsenal of conquered worlds, giving him an advantage in future battles. However, he desired their unique energy source most of all, and he was already planning to incorporate the energy source into his fleet and himself on a cellular level. He had devised a plan to use the energy to increase his direct energy attacks and thus become more powerful.

His plan would require some assistance from the Nagapie, as AnaTi wasn't aware that the type of energy from the Nagapie could exist outside the body. His race were only able to generate energy from within themselves, and that was a taxing feat to perform.

The night before his descent, Trix and Hilee went outside their home to gaze at the stars, trying to ease their troubled minds. They held each other tightly as the night breeze rustled through their fluffy tails.

THE FOLLOWING MORNING AnaTi descended onto the Nagapie planet like a great thunderstorm. The sky was darkened by his fleet, loud noises filled the air, and vibrations shook the ground. There was no escape from the malignant threat that was on the Nagapie's doorstep. The battle cruisers were too big to land on the city of VanBo, so they landed in a circle on the ground around the city. AnaTi made sure there was a lot of collateral damage during his descent, enough to instil deep fear into the Nagapie.

Thousands of hectares of forest were destroyed in an instant, crushed by the heat and sheer mass of the fleet. Shortly after touching down on the planet, AnaTi emerged from his ship, flying on his own up to the city to engage with the Nagapies. The timid creatures were gathered outside the tallest building, with the Chieftain spearheading the masses to establish contact. AnaTi touched down on the surface of the city, facing the small Chieftain. The air was filled with the disgusting smell of sulphur, which was his natural odour.

Not a single sound was made by the Nagapie.

The Chieftain worked up the courage to walk over to AnaTi and presented him with a small device to be placed on AnaTi's head. It was a translating device that would allow basic communication between species. The Chieftain showed AnaTi that he was also wearing one to get AnaTi to use it. Once AnaTi placed the device on his head, the

Chieftain started the dialogue. 'Greetings, Tall Lord. Why did you come to our world with such a destructive force?'

'I want your energy source that powers your civilisation,' AnaTi responded in short.

That was when the Chieftain realised that the energy source, once seen as a symbol of hope, progress, and advancement, could be used to bring destruction and chaos.

'We do not possess the skills to recreate or do anything with the energy,' the Chieftain lied. 'It was created by our forefathers, and they did not share that knowledge with us.'

'That truly is bad news,' AnaTi responded sarcastically. 'Then I will have to force you to regain that knowledge for me.'

And with that short dialogue, the negotiations were over. Not that the Nagapies had a fair chance to start with.

AnaTi signalled his fleet to execute their attack. The primate species was overpowered and enslaved within a few hours. Their physical stature and love of peace made them a soft target for the tyrant and they had little chance to defend or rebel against their new master. But over the next few days of silent suffering, they formed a plan to deliver them and the galaxy from this evil.

Using their telepathy, they engaged and debated how to overcome such a powerful and fearsome enemy. After days of reasoning using collective telepathy, a solution was obtained. They needed to create a saviour, not an equal to this threat, but something far greater and stronger. AnaTi was unaware of the telepathic abilities and under the guise of rediscovering the origins of their energy source, they looked to genetic enactments for this purpose, hoping they could alter one of their own kind to be their saviour and hero. They made huge strides in gathering DNA data and splicing it, they managed to collect data from every warrior slave in AnaTi's fleet, including AnaTi himself.

The enhanced DNA was refined and built over and over until they found a perfect solution. The base of the DNA structure was that of a primate, a humanoid mammal, with the design of being compatible with themselves. With their advanced technology, they managed to increase the number of chromosomes in the DNA structure and even code their energy source as separate chromosomes. This would allow their saviour to generate energy within and also focus it into direct energy attacks, like the skills possessed by AnaTi. They also added memory to the structure, giving the recipient generational background and emotions about the creators and the evil of their time.

However, the solution was purely in data form, as they had no physical sample to use. And it was difficult to create a sample with their master and his soldiers' watchful eyes monitoring them all day long. Eventually, they devised a plan to create two samples, one to be used on their planet and one to be sent into the galaxy as hope for other planets and life. They convinced their master that they needed to use a laboratory for a possible new strength serum that would make AnaTi physically stronger. This idea appealed to the tyrant, and he permitted them to carry on with the experiment and research.

The solution was simple; a single cell, that once injected into its host, would multiply and change the DNA structure of the host to produce the new all-powerful being. Our scientific interpretation of this solution would be comparable to that of a virus, which would infect and alter its host.

The two samples were created under great secrecy and deceit. One of the samples was placed in a syringe, to be administrated to one of the Nagapie. They had selected a member amongst them who had no children in case something went wrong. The second sample was placed in a protective casing shaped like a dagger's blade. Once the second sample was placed into the casing, the tip was sealed.

Administrating the second sample would require the tip to be removed and injecting it into the host. The casing had a translucent green appearance, almost see-through like tinted glass. The dagger's blade had a seal on the end to protect the sample. The blade was placed in a tube container, and a compact version of its unique energy source was placed at the bottom of the tube to create a hypersonic rocket.

AFTER FIVE MONTHS IN captivity, the Nagapies set their plan into motion. The plan was to use both samples at once, the local injection and the space-bound blade. Once they had set coordinates to a distant galaxy for the rocket, they proceeded to inject the Nagapie member selected for this crucial task. It was Hilee. Because she could not bear any younglings for Trix, the collective sought her as the best candidate. To Hilee this seemed like a death sentence by her own kind. She did not want this to happen to her. She wanted a normal and happy life with Trix. But it was not meant for her.

Hilee's transformation started instantly, as she fell to the floor and started worming around in agonising pain. At that point, the rocket took off with a flash of light. It moved so fast that it looked like lighting was shot up from the ground. Unfortunately, the rocket raised the alarm with their capturers, and their location was stormed immediately. The guards seized the Nagapie in the laboratory, except for Hilee who was nowhere to be found. Hilee had disappeared and has still not been seen to this very day.

The Nagapies got away with their experiment as there was no proof of any wrongdoing. Nowhere was there a trace of meddling with DNA or any sample. They explained to their captors that the bright light was an accident in the lab that had set off a reaction. Though there was no proof of foul play, AnaTi was furious with their failure to provide him the promised strength serum, so he ordered the slaughter of the Nagapies who had worked on the project. To AnaTi's later regret, he realised he had wiped out most of the elders from the Nagapie race, which left them without the knowledge to recreate their unique energy source. However, AnaTi continued to make use of their home world and started turning it into his base of operations.

THE ROCKET WITH THE blade inside was now travelling far, in and out of galaxies. As chance would have it, it made contact with an asteroid in our solar system which sent the rocket tumbling to earth. As the tumbling rocket entered Earth's atmosphere most of the rocket started to burn up because of the high speed and friction in Earth's atmosphere. It came shooting down into Africa, central Africa, now known as the Congo (DRC). The object was not detected by the Earth's satellites due to its small size and velocity. It hit the ground during the year 1994, while the region was in turmoil due to the Rwanda Genocide.

The falling object was noticed by militia members of the extremist group Hutu. They saw the falling object at close range and where it had made an impact. Their leader took a handful of soldiers to go and investigate, initially thinking it was a rocket from their opposition, the Tutsi militia. Upon investigating the crash site, they discovered the unworldly object – a dagger blade that was glowing bright green from the heat in between the debris. The Hutu leader saw this as a sign, that the gods had sent them a magical weapon of power. Although they would never find out and truly comprehend the true power of the green blade, they carefully removed the glowing object from the debris and took it to their general, who was behind the massacre in the region.

Looking at the blade, they attached their own superstition to it, believing that it would bring power and victory to the extremist. The general of the militia had an ivory handle made for the blade to suit his hand and grip. He had it engraved with skulls in a pattern and the phrase, Night of the Long Knives. A sheath was made from lion skin, with gold droplets burnt into the skin and raw diamonds placed along the outer edges. The dagger grew in reputation as the genocide continued and the Hutu slayed about one million of the minority Tutsi group.

The dagger became one of the most sought-after artefacts in the underground world, as different extremist groups started to believe in its power. The dagger moved around the Congo, the Middle East, and back to Africa as it was sold and moved amongst Islamic extremists. By the year 2024, the dagger had seen so much blood that the handle was stained deep red, though the blade retained its translucent green lustre.

The current owner of the dagger was the leader of ISIS-M, Koji Bemin. He came into possession of the dagger in 2017 when it was sent to him from the Middle East to wish him success in his campaign. And ever since then, the dagger had hung around his neck, like a gold medallion won at the Olympics. Like the dagger's previous earthly owners, it was used to instil fear and used as a ceremonial tool when Koji carried out his executions of innocent people. His blood lust grew ever stronger with each throat that he slit and with each heart that he stabbed.

Chapter 7

The sun rose slowly on the next day of the terrorists holding the hostages. For most it was not a sign of hope. The hostages were exhausted; they had barely slept since their capture nor eaten anything. In the early light, the hostages noticed that the terrorists were moving around a lot more than a few hours ago. It looked as though they were preparing for something. Vani thought it was a sign that perhaps the government was trying to take back the area, which was bound to happen at some stage. The captain who had caught the three businessmen was moving up and down between the various floors, barking orders and instructions.

The captain engaged briefly with one of the guards during a trip down the flight of stairs. 'We must move quickly; the Mozambique government is sending the army here. We must do the broadcasting now. I'm just getting the main gate ready for an assault. After the broadcasts we will move to our headquarters.'

Benjamin could understand what he was saying, but he did not pass the message to the others, as they were forbidden to speak, and he feared another beating or worse. He did find it odd that their current location wasn't their headquarters, considering the scale of the operations and how organised they were.

The terrorists had finished setting up their broadcasting room, which was previously the board room where the three businessmen had held their customer meeting the previous day. The room had a camera in the front centre with a laptop and router behind it. All the windows were blacked out and pieces of fabric and at the back of the room hung an ISIS banner with some text below it, indicating that the terrorist group was a branch of the larger ISIS group that was known throughout the Western world.

Their plan was to bring in four to five hostages at a time and have them state their name, occupancy, and country of origin; following that, the general would inform the viewers that the hostages could be released if a ransom amount of one million US dollars each was paid. Some would be killed during the broadcast to show their intent and that they were not to be taken lightly. There was no pattern as to who would die, it would all depend on how the general felt about someone. The terrorists were well organised for the live-streaming event, they had several channels to which it would be streamed, with banking and payment details shown throughout the event. Links to their various channels were sent to a comprehensive list of newspapers throughout the world.

And so, it started. The captain instructed the guards to bring up the first five hostages. The guards strode into the group and took five people with force, creating panic and confusion amongst the hostages. The prisoners were clinging to each other for dear life, so much so that more guards had to step in to separate the people. The first five were shoved up the stairs to the broadcasting room. The general sat on a chair at the side of the room waiting for them.

'Line them up against the flag,' he ordered the guards.

The hostages were lined up side by side with a guard behind each of them pointing their cleaned rifles at the hostages. The hostages faced the camera as the general gave them instructions.

'Now, you will state your name, job, and country. Then we will take you back to the other hostages. If your government likes you, they will pay us for your release. You see, it is not us that keeps you here, but it is your different governments' willingness to pay.'

The hostages stood trembling in absolute fear. A terrorist in charge of the camera gave a sign to the general to indicate that the live streaming had started. All over the world, various newspaper journalists joined the streaming to see what scoop they could get for tomorrow's paper. The general stepped in front of the hostages and faced the camera to make his statement and demand.

'Yesterday, we, as ISIS-M, freed a region in our home country from the corrupt infidels that took our freedom. Today the governments of these thieves will pay us to ensure the return of their people. If we don't get paid, you don't get your people; it is that simple. To show we are serious, I will use the holy blade to kill one out of every five hostages. That is my sacrifice to the almighty Allah. There is no negotiating around my sacrifice.' As the general spoke, he pulled the green dagger from its sheath and held it up high in the air for the entire world to see.

He stepped closer to the hostages and told them to begin. The first person was a man from China, he did not understand Portuguese or English, and in a panic, he tried to explain that he didn't understand in Mandarin. It was bad luck for the Chinese man because this infuriated the general. The general slowly moved closer to the Chinese man, leaned in close, almost face to face, and stabbed him in the solar plexus with the dagger. He twisted the dagger to see the excruciating pain on the Chinese man's face, and then he yanked the dagger free, causing the Chinese man to die almost immediately. The general ordered two guards to remove the corpse and take it to the burial site. The other four hostages from the first group got the opportunity to state their information as demanded by the general.

After the first round, the stream was stopped, and the remaining four hostages were transported back to the holding room. However, they were kept separate from the large group so the terrorists could keep track of who still had to speak. When the next five hostages were brought up to the broadcasting room, the general moved his chair from the side to the middle.

He wanted to be more in the spotlight, and he started doing something that none of the dagger's previous owners had ever done. He wanted to create a dramatic effect, build tension, and feed his ego. So, he took out a sharpening stone to sharpen the dagger, which no one had ever done because the blade never dulled. He started grinding the dagger from the bottom of the blade to the top, in a half circle motion. With each grinding movement, the seal that kept the modified DNA inside was loosened, little by little.

———————✶✶————————

THE TERRORISTS WENT through six groups, meaning six people were murdered through the livestream. The larger group soon noticed after the third round of hostages had been returned, that there was one person short each time and they concluded that one in five were killed. This made the hostages even more anxious each time the guards came to collect new hostages.

In the seventh round, the guards took Vani and Jacob with three other nationals from the UK. The UK hostages kicked and screamed as much as possible, which only made the guards use more force. Vani moved slowly due to his sprained ankle, and this was also seen as a delaying tactic by the guards. One of the guards took the rifle off his shoulder and hit Vani on the head with the back end of his weapon. Blood gushed from the wound and ran down Vani's face. Then two guards picked Vani up by the arms and dragged him up the stairs to the broadcasting room.

By this time, the live streaming of the hostage scenario went viral around the world. Various governments tried to shut the links down in their respective countries, to prevent people from seeing the gruesome executions. However, most news agencies kept the stream going, to identify the hostages and which countries they were from. It was a traumatic event to witness, the world felt sympathy for the hostages and what was happening to them.

There was immediate global political pressure on the Mozambique government, with all the countries wanting answers. However, the Mozambique government had been just as surprised by the site invasion and scale of the terrorist operations. Many countries with citizens caught as hostages started to mobilise efforts to start a rescue mission, while other countries condemned the attack and voiced their intentions to support the Mozambique army. Countries closer to Mozambique started preparing to deploy their troops to aid the army's attempt to retake the mining site.

The seventh set of hostages was lined up, and they placed Vani first in line. The general sat on his chair, admiring the dagger as he ran it over the grinding stone. The green glow from the dagger had faded under the blood that had dried on it.

Unknowingly, the general had ground off the seal on the dagger with his last stroke, exposing the enhanced DNA now ready for administration. The general got up from his chair and made his way to Vani.

'I remember you. I was waiting for you. I saw you stare at my dagger earlier; do you know it's special?'

The general stared at Vani, waiting for an answer, but Vani was still dazed and confused from the blow to his head.

'You don't want to speak, even now when they may be your last words? Where are you from?'

Vani stared at the general through his left eye, as the right was closed to prevent blood from flowing into it.

'South Africa, jou doos,' Vani muttered.

The general's bloodshot eyes widened with excitement. 'You are my first South African! I remember the stories of your people, the strong military you had, the resilience of your nation. And now, now you are nothing, just a joke.'

The general slid the dagger across Vani's cheek, and another stream of blood appeared instantly. 'I will take magnificent pleasure in showing the world that you South Africans are nothing! You have no legend because you no longer have a country.'

It wasn't blind hatred that filled Vani, instead, he was filled with great sadness. Sad because he knew that he would never see his beautiful daughters again. They would grow up without him there to teach them all the things he still wanted them to know. A tear started running down his cheek and mixed with the blood from the cut. Vani said a silent prayer. 'Look after my children, please my Lord. Be there for them when I am no longer here.'

The general mistook this as a sign of weakness, he thought that he had broken Vani's spirit. 'Bwhaahaaahaaa, you see, you cry like a little girl!' He grabbed Vani's face by the jaw and turned him towards the camera. 'You see, World, this is what became of your once-mighty nation! Crying like a baby!'

And then Vani turned his head away from the general, lifted his chin proudly, and closed his eyes. He began to hum a melody, which turned into a soft mumbling of lyrics and then he began to sing with his whole heart. His voice was deep, changing the entire mood in the room. The general had no idea what he was singing, but he was stunned into silence.

> 'Uit die blou van onse hemel,
> Uit die diepte van ons see,
> Oor ons ewige gebergtes
> Waar die kranse antwoord gee.
> Deur ons vêr-verlate vlaktes
> Met die kreun van ossewa –
> Ruis die stem van ons geliefde,
> Van ons land Suid-Afrika.'

In a massive fit of anger, the general launched forward with all his strength and plunged the dagger straight into Vani's heart. In that instant of rage, the advanced DNA was transferred into Vani's body. Vani coughed up a large amount of blood before visibly weakening. The guard who was behind Vani holding him dropped his lifeless body to the floor.

Suddenly, a dark cloud grew rapidly out of nowhere. The clouds started moving in a spiral shape, creating a vortex of clouds above the building. High winds collided with the building corners, creating loud howling noises. A lightning storm started up; lighting bolts formed a web around the building. The broadcast room with the blacked-out windows turned even darker. The terrorist soldiers froze in the room, they were struck with fear. Lighting crashed around them. And then in a loud and blinding flash, a lightning bolt struck Vani's body. The room was filled with such a white bright light that no one could see anything, not even the camera lens nor the viewers on the other side of the camera.

As the bright light persisted, Vani's body began levitating off the ground. All the light got sucked into Vani's body in an instant, and then a massive energy wave burst shot out of him and travelled in a spherical shape outward, from Earth into space. The energy wave was so strong that it moved and disorientated every satellite in Earth's orbit. Astronauts on the international space station saw the event and recalled it as an anomaly that looked like a massive explosion of light happening on the surface of the planet.

When the freak storm dissipated everyone in the broadcasting room was silent. Stares of disbelief were exchanged around the room, no one knew what had just happened. Then Jacob looked down at Vani's lifeless body lying on the floor and he broke the strange silence.

'No! Vani! You fucking bastards!'

The general was also dumbstruck, he felt his hand that had stabbed Vani shaking to the bone. The dagger, which had now served its purpose, had completely lost its green glow. It had also lost most of its weight, as the DNA that was transferred into Vani had the weight of a super-heavy element. Furious that the dagger had lost its appeal, the general ordered two guards to take Vani's body to the burial site.

THE BURIAL SITE WAS nothing more than a deep ditch next to the office block which was being used as a mass grave. There were already a lot of bodies in the ditch, everyone that had been killed during the mining invasion had been dumped there. By the time Vani's body was thrown in, it was already swarming with flies and a foul stench surrounded the area. The heat provided the perfect breeding ground for this horrific sight. Corpses were just thrown on top of each other, and despite the heat, the large volume of spilt blood did not evaporate. After the incident with Vani, the general lost his temper completely and began killing hostages at random. There were about twenty more bodies piled on top of Vani that day.

TWO DAYS AFTER THE broadcast of Vani's murder, the local news in South Africa announced at 19:00 that they had confirmed he was indeed in the area and presumed dead. As with such news, no one wants to say outright that someone is dead without official proof. It was during this news broadcast that South Africans were shocked and heartbroken to learn of the incident. His daughters were distraught and shattered when learning the news from their mother.

Chapter 8

With quickly growing confidence, fame, and followers, the terrorists decided it was time to move on to bigger things. They were going to abandon the mining site and invade a large town close by, Tete. The town was much larger than Moatize and offered more options for gaining power and accumulating resources. The mining site would retain some military presence; however, the bulk of their forces would move to Tete which had been scouted with battle plans drawn up months in advance.

The day after Vani's execution the terrorist group started mobilising their forces to move out. The whole office block on the mining site which they had occupied was cleared out, they left only twenty soldiers at the main gate to create a distraction when needed. The mass grave was left unattended.

Maggots started to breed in the corpses in the mass grave. The flies swarmed above, creating a black cloud. The smell of rotting flesh travelled far, drawing in other scavengers. Crows and vultures came to feast on the soft flesh, and by nightfall, some corpses had their faces pecked clean of skin, eyes, lips, and noses. The local authorities were engaged in several battles in the area; however, they could not reach the mining site and so the number of dead people and their names could not be determined.

FIFTEEN KILOMETRES west of the mine was a small rural village of about eighty people with three members who worked on the mining site. The village had mostly elderly people and young children, there were few working adults. Thus, the villagers' concern grew as the days went by and there was no news about the three men from the village who worked for various contractors at the mine. On Saturday, the village had a council meeting, where they discussed their options and decided that they would need to send a search party to the site, to look for their bodies and any possible signs of life.

It was agreed that seven members from the village would make up the search party, four men and three women. They would set out in the dark of Sunday morning to get into the site undetected. At around 03:00 Sunday morning, they left the village, only taking linen, ropes, and long poles that could be used to construct three stretchers. They travelled as lightly as possible, with the hope of bringing some people back home.

Their journey was silent, not a word was spoken over the entire fifteen kilometres. They arrived at the mining site with some cover of the night sky left. The villagers got access to the mining site where the fence had been dropped because of an agreement between the mine and the rural village, to grant them extra grazing ground for their cattle. Very few people knew of this access point to the mining site. Still in darkness, they moved towards the workshop, not knowing where to start searching. As they got closer there were no terrorists in sight, which gave them a feeling of relief. A feeling that left instantly when the smell of rotting bodies reached them.

The villagers moved quickly and silently, following their noses in the direction of the stench. None of them had ever been to this part of the mining site, they'd always avoided the busy areas. As they exited the workshop, they saw the tall office blocks, where they paused to look around. The office buildings looked ominous and made them uneasy. Though the buildings were deserted, there was a lingering presence of the evil that had been there not too long ago.

They started moving out of the cover of the workshop towards the buildings. Under the dim light of the starry sky, they spotted the mass grave in the ditch next to one of the office buildings. Moving closer they began to distance themselves from any hope of finding survivors. Now standing on the edge of the ditch, they saw that it was almost filled to the brim with corpses. The women among them grabbed their mouths to prevent their screams of horror escaping. Two of the men fell to their knees; they could not comprehend such malice.

The oldest man amongst them, known as Solly, gave steady whispered instructions. 'Let's make two groups, we'll pull bodies out from the ditch and try to find our brothers and sisters.' And so, the villagers started to pull body after body out of the ditch. They had removed twenty-three bodies in total, when they came to Vani's body. Two men pulled him by his arms and dragged him out of the ditch. On the top, they dropped his body on the ground and turned to continue their search.

Then to everyone's fright, they heard a muffled cough. The villagers stared in fear at the row of bodies, holding their breath in anticipation of another sound. They immediately froze in position, thinking the spirits of the dead were angry and talking. But when there was no other sound, they sighed and continued pulling bodies out. They placed the corpses next to each other in a single row to make sure they didn't overlook anyone.

Another ten minutes went by when they heard another cough. This time they did not confuse it with a spirit trying to communicate, it was a clear cough. As the group stood by nervously, Solly walked along the row of bodies, checking each one more carefully. And then Vani moved his arm.

With excitement, they rushed to investigate his state. Solly instructed another man and woman to help him move Vani into a spot that had more light and asked the rest of the team to continue with the search. After dragging Vani into the light, Solly listened for breathing and checked for a heartbeat. He could barely detect a heartbeat, but Vani was breathing. He tore open Vani's shirt to look at his injury, and gasped in shock at the large wound in his chest from the stabbing. What shocked Solly was how the wound had filled up with a glowing green tissue. 'We have to save this man,' Solly said to the other two. 'He will come back with us. For now, let's continue the search. He has survived till now; he will not die here.'

The villagers continued with their search and before reaching the bottom of the ditch they found all three of the men from their village. Their corpses brought great sorrow to the search party, but for now, they had the comfort of closure. 'We will mourn our dead at home and give them proper burials,' Solly said. They constructed three stretchers with the material they had brought with them. Two of the deceased were placed on a single stretcher, and the third body and Vani were placed on their own stretchers. They tied the bodies and Vani to the stretchers to prevent them from falling off during transportation.

The villagers started their journey back with the sun almost at its high point. They left the site as they had entered it, unnoticed, quickly, and quietly. The sun was beating down on them, sweat was dripping off Vani and it was clear he was in severe pain.

THEY REACHED THEIR village in the late afternoon, where they were greeted by screams of grief as the villagers saw the bodies of the dead. The three stretchers were laid down in the middle of the village and the mourning wives, mothers, and children surrounded the dead bodies of their loved ones. One of the village elders, named Willy, looked at Vani in amazement. 'How is this man still alive and why did you bring him here, Solly?

Solly explained the conditions in which they had found Vani and their dead villagers. 'He was thrown out just like our brothers, like a pile of trash. The terrorists treated everyone like they meant nothing. When

I saw him alive with that wound, I knew there was something different about this man.'

Willy gave Solly a glare. 'What if the terrorists come here looking for him?'

'They won't,' Solly replied. 'He was thrown out like a corpse, amongst the other corpses. They think he is dead and it does look like he was dead for a while. No one will come looking for him.'

Willy gave it some thought and agreed that Vani could stay until he was able to move. There was nowhere the villagers could take Vani for help. The two closest towns were occupied by terrorists, and the roads leading to them were a constant war zone. The decision was made, they would shelter Vani and try to keep him alive until he could leave on his own.

Vani was placed in Solly's hut where Solly's family would look after Vani. For the first week, they tried to keep Vani cool with wet cloths and fed him water. Keeping Vani hydrated wasn't an easy task, as he was comatose. They lifted his head and poured tiny amounts of water into his mouth. The wound on Vani's chest was closing fast with what now appeared to be normal flesh and skin.

Solly noticed that Vani's body was undergoing some other changes. During the first week, Vani's appearance of muscle and muscle mass increased. He also noticed changes in his physical size, as his shoulders, hands, and feet grew wider and wider, which didn't make sense, as he wasn't eating or moving. Solly's wife also started to comment on the weight of Vani's head. She was the person giving him water daily, and she noticed it had become increasingly more difficult to lift his head. They also noticed the grass reed mat and the ground that he was sleeping on were flattened as if they were supporting a heavy weight. They couldn't understand nor explain what they were witnessing.

What was happening was the start of the transformation. The modified DNA that had been engineered by the Nagapie was starting to change Vani's body. Because of certain similarities between the human DNA and that of the Nagapie, the transformation process was working. Vani's DNA was being rewritten with version two-point-o, and the structure itself became denser with the added modifications. His bone structure began expanding and grew much denser and harder, to the point where it was comparable with solid nanofiber structures. There was additional bone structure being formed, three extra rib bones grew in his rib cage on either side. And around his heart, a protective mesh casing formed, like the skull protecting the brain. The spine changed as well; all the vertebrae grew extra masses in the shape of small shark fins to protect the spine better.

His muscles also changed drastically, not just in shape and weight, but also in function. The muscles were transformed into powerful biological batteries that stored the unique energy the Nagapie had created. This energy was generated within his body and stored mostly in his muscles. As with the bones and muscles, his skin also became tougher and smarter. The skin had become tougher than Kevlar in terms of cut resistance and extremely hard to pierce. His skin behaved like a non-Newtonian fluid, whereby it was soft and flexible under normal conditions, but the cells hardened when pressure or heat was applied. It also inherited regenerative capabilities, which allowed it to heal almost instantly. His skin now had the natural ability to blend in with his environment, as adaptive camouflage was part of the sampling pool for the engineered DNA.

Vani's senses were also enhanced, and a few new senses were added. His standard five human senses were all heightened and sharpened. He no longer needed to wear his glasses and his eyesight also included more spectrums of visibility; he could see heat signatures, and magnetic fields, and had perfect night vision. Added senses were the ability to feel and sense energy sources, telepathy, and memory scanning of other living beings.

During the second week, they noticed that Vani was starting to drift in and out of his coma, which they took as a good sign. Solly thought it would be now a suitable time to consult with Willy on what they had been observing. He called Willy into his hut to show him, he started with the wound that had now completely healed up. Willy stood wide-eyed and in silence while Solly pointed out the changes. 'I have never seen a wound heal so quickly or someone becoming stronger just by sleeping,' Solly said. 'Do you think it has something to do with him being a white person?'

Willy shifted his glare to Solly. 'How can you be so old and still speak such nonsense?'

Willy took a deep breath and then gave his opinion. 'They say the terrorist leader has a magical dagger that he uses to kill these people. A dagger sent from the stars. I believe he used that dagger to kill this man and in doing so, the magic left the dagger and found itself a new host. The magic that lived within the dagger now lives in this human.' Solly felt ashamed for his account of the situation, questioning his maturity.

'Truly you were meant to bring him here to our village, that much is clear to me now. He will play a big part in our salvation from the terrorists that have been slaughtering our people,' Willy said calmly. 'We must take good care of him, let him understand we are on the same side once he wakes up.'

IN THE SECOND WEEK Vani began hearing the village sounds when he was conscious. He heard voices and discussions during the day and an FM radio during the night. He was having lucid and graphic dreams of an evil creature hunting him. The villagers noted his restlessness and wondered what haunted his dreams. Their interpretation was that he was still fighting with the terrorists in his head.

The truth behind it was much more intense for Vani. Amongst all the changes and growing pains, the mental changes were the most intense. His brain matter expanded only slightly, but despite the small change, the impact was massive. Coupled with the change to his brain were the DNA memories the Nagapie had built into the DNA structure – similar to the inherent memories we get from our forefathers but just more complete; it included intel and background on AnaTi and the Nagapie race. Creatures that Vani could never comprehend or imagine were being imprinted into his permanent memories. It was a great struggle for the human mind to deal with this new reality and to accept it. Vani's enhanced senses also caused a lot of shock and confusion and his brain had to recalibrate itself to the heightened senses to gain control over them.

AT THE END OF THE SECOND week, Vani started moving his digits. First were the fingers on his right hand, then the fingers on his left hand, and last he managed to move his toes. His brain and body underwent massive changes, and it was doing start-up procedures, by checking if his digits were functioning correctly. The villagers were excited to see this and it became each morning's main topic of discussion when villagers would ask Solly what new improvement he had noticed.

Back in South Africa, the country was still in shock over the terrorist attacks so close to home. It had been exceedingly difficult for Vani's two girls to accept the news of his death. They loved their pappa very much. Astrid, who was the most attached to her father, refused to accept the news and believed if she prayed hard enough her pappa would return soon.

Vani's Ex was preparing her attorneys to lay claim to Vani's assets and pension funds. She spent her nights greedily calculating what she could gain financially from Vani's demise.

Saskia felt deep sorrow. She had lost a part of her life, a part of her history.

Vani's family was also devastated as they tried to sort out the administrative side of his death. This proved to be a nightmare as many institutions and authorities required a death certificate, which was not yet available.

The company where Vani worked assisted his family as best they could, but as it usually goes within any big organisation, others gradually took over his projects, and life in the corporate world went on without him.

Chapter 9

During the third week Vani spent in the village, he started recovering a lot faster. His body had now adapted to most of the changes and his mental state was more stable. On the Monday morning of the third week, Vani lay on his back, looking at the thatched roof of the hut. He understood he had been taken care of, that some of the local people must have rescued him. However, he couldn't recall much between when he was stabbed and the present day.

Gazing at the different shades of brown grass above, it suddenly hit him. A massive feeling of longing. Longing to be with his children. He thought of them, and tears started running down the side of his face. These heartfelt emotions were quickly replaced by a drive to get back to them. A drive to get back at the evil that had almost robbed him of being with his children. In that moment Vani found his motivation to get back onto his feet. He slowly rolled onto his side to support his weight with his arm. Solly saw this and ran out of the hut shouting joyfully, 'He is getting up, he is moving!'

The villagers come running to Solly's hut and formed a crowd in front of the door, everyone trying to get a look at this man who had miraculously recovered from almost certain death. Most of the chatter was in Portuguese and Vani didn't understand a word. Vani pushed himself upright and now for the first time he was able to see his body. He was dumbstruck by all the changes. He looked at his hands, and flexed his fingers, feeling their strength. Staring down at his chest, he noticed there was extraordinarily little scar tissue where he had been stabbed. Vani touched his face to feel his beard, to get an indication of how long he had been unconscious. Strangely he found that his beard had not grown much since he was stabbed.

As the inherent memories trickled through his mind, Vani understood that his body had been changed for a purpose. Though he was still not aware of what his new body was capable of, he felt that he would be instrumental in rescuing his friends and liberating the country's people from the terrorists.

Willy and Solly squeezed through the crowd at the doorway to get inside the hut with Vani, and immediately started speaking.

Vani held up his hands to stop them. 'Sorry, I don't understand Portuguese, does anyone speak English?'

Solly shook his head sadly. 'Right now, I am the only person left in the village that speaks some English. We had three other members that could also speak English, but they were killed in the attack on the mining site. Do you know your name and where you are and what happened to you at the mine?'

'Uhhhmm... my name is Vani, Vani van der Merwe. I'm from South Africa. There was an attack at the mine, we tried to escape... have you seen any of my colleagues!?' Vani asked.

'No, you would have to go back to the mass grave at the mine to search for your colleagues,' said Solly. 'We found you alive while searching for our brothers. You have been healing for more than two weeks, but remembering your initial wound, you should be dead. Why are you not dead? How did you grow bigger and heavier by just resting? There is something strange about you.'

Vani looked at his chest and his forearms – now more muscular than ever before – and replied, 'I have no idea what has happened. This body of mine feels new to me. I wasn't built like this before I got stabbed. Something must have changed. It feels like I did a massive amount of exercise, like my muscles are in a recovery phase. And there is something else about my body, I don't know what, but something bizarre, I can't quite explain it. A strange warmth from inside me. Why would this happen to me?'

Vani paused as a cold chill came over him, he had goosebumps in the heat of Mozambique. He muttered a word that none of the men had ever heard before. 'AnaTi.'

Solly asked, 'What are you saying now? I don't understand this word.'

'Neither do I, but it unsettles me to think of it,' Vani responded. 'What happened to the terrorists, and the mining site, were there any survivors?'

Solly took a seat next to Vani on the ground and looked at him as he gathered himself. 'We were all caught off guard by the surprise attack, but even if we knew it was coming, there would've been very little we could have done, except to keep our brothers at home. The attack on the mine was quick, no one saw it coming, and after a few days the bad men left the site with only a few guards. They attacked the town of Moatize, killed, raped, burned, and stole what they could. It seems they only wanted to see Moatize burned down. From Moatize they moved to Tete. We hear that there has been heavy fighting in Tete, with a lot of people trying to fight back. But the bad men now control the city, which means they control the area from the mining site to Tete. Their numbers are growing by the day.'

Solly stopped his conversation to ask one of the villagers standing by the door to get some water for him and Vani. After taking a sip he continued, 'Some of the people that they have captured are still being held captive. They keep the foreigners alive to get ransom for their release and they use our local people to increase their numbers. They use the men and boys as soldiers. While imprisoned, they give them drugs, making addicts out of them and telling them that they will get more drugs if our people fight for them. We heard they also promise lots of money, fame, and women.' Solly composed himself again.

'It is with this knowledge that we are more grateful that our brothers have died rather than been turned into terrorists, beasts, and murderers, for some things are worse to accept than death. Our military and police cannot break through the defensive lines the bad men have put up; they fight but nothing changes for us here on the wrong side of the line. Our food is running low, we are living off the little that we grow and what we can find in nature.'

Then Solly's grim face lightened. 'But Vani, what will you do now? Will you help us, or will you try and make it back to your own country? Keep in mind you are far away from home.'

'Indeed, I am, and I wish that I could be back home with my children. I have two daughters,' Vani answered. 'Can you give me some more time to rest, please? I'm feeling very tired, and I would like to think over my options now that I know what my current situation is.'

Solly had been hoping to get an answer immediately; considering the village's current situation they were all desperate for some glimmer of hope. 'Of course, you may take some time to think about it. I will go look for some clothes that will fit you.' Solly got up and left the hut. He spoke outside with the villagers asking for large men's clothing and a bucket with warm water and soap.

He returned shortly and handed Vani the clothes and the bucket. 'Here, this should get the dirt and old blood off you.' He closed the door behind him to give Vani some privacy.

For the first time in over two weeks, Vani stood on his own two feet. He peeled his old clothes off, they were torn, smelled bad, and were stained with blood. He stood for a while, further inspecting how his body had changed. He pressed with his index finger on the scar on his chest, expecting to feel a jolt of pain, but there was nothing, the wound wasn't sensitive. He stretched out his limbs and took a deep breath. Then he noticed something else that was bizarre, he could just keep on breathing like he didn't have limited lung capacity. Eventually after about a minute, he stopped breathing in, suddenly paranoid that he might pop like a balloon.

Vani knelt at the bucket to wash himself and the familiar position reminded him.

Ah yes, how could I be so careless and forget the first thing I should've done after waking up, he thought. He straightened his upper body, put his hands together, and started praying. His prayer was made up of three main topics. First, he thanked the Lord repeatedly for giving him a second chance and for keeping him safe. Secondly, he prayed for his children to be safe and for the Lord to protect them. And thirdly he asked for guidance, knowledge, and wisdom to help determine what he should do next.

After his prayer, he washed and put on the clean clothes. Feeling refreshed but still fatigued, he went to lie down on the straw mat which had been his bed for more than two weeks. At this point, his body was used to sleeping on the hard ground and a small wood bench for a pillow.

WITHOUT INTENDING TO, Vani fell asleep for two full days. When he woke, the door of the hut was open, it was still morning, and the villagers were going about their daily business. He got up and walked outside. Looking up at the sky he was amazed by how blue and clear it was. The children in the village ran up to him, chanting his name and touching him. He looked at them and smiled, the friendliness was a welcome change from his recent experience.

He walked with the children over to where Solly was busy piling wood.

'I have my answer to your question from the other day,' Vani said to Solly. 'Both questions.'

'What do you mean by both, my friend?' Solly asked with a puzzled look.

'I will help you, try to find my friends, and then make my way back home. I see these events as interlinked; I need to repay you for saving me and I must discover what has happened to my friends, otherwise, I will not be able to live with myself and look my children in the eye. One event leads to the next, and I believe it happened this way for a reason, and my body has changed for a reason. Do you know where they might be keeping the hostages, where have they moved them to?'

Solly replied, 'I do not know the exact place, all I know is that they have set up camp in an abandoned small school next to the road just outside Tete. You should go look there. Just how exactly are you planning to help us?'

'By cutting off the head of the snake,' replied Vani, 'I will kill the leader of the terrorist group and kill as many of his soldiers as I possibly can. Then I will look for my friends and start moving back home. I plan to leave at nightfall and doubt you will see me for a long time. Just know, that when their leader is killed and this terror ends, it was you who helped me to do it.'

Solly leaned forward and embraced Vani. 'Thank you, my friend,' he said, 'Willy believed you were sent here to deliver us from this evil. Thank you.'

After their conversation, the two men went to eat. They sat in front of a smouldering fire which was keeping a large black cast-iron pot warm. Solly took a plate and dished up a portion of maize meal from the large pot. He handed Vani some strips of dried-out beef, which had been preserved like biltong. Vani was famished. The food was basic but it didn't take away from the fact that Vani enjoyed the meal. He wanted to ask for a second helping, but looking around he could see the villagers had little to eat, so he refrained from asking.

The rest of the day was spent with Vani answering some of the villagers' questions, with the aid of Solly translating for everyone. Interestingly, the villagers were more curious about Vani's life back in

South Africa, rather than the incident he had survived. They were keen to learn about his way of life and what life was like in a big city.

As the night approached, the villagers grew quieter. Solly explained it was out of fear for the terrorists. Generally, they would still be active till about ten pm, engaging in group activities and conversations around the bonfire. However, since the attacks began, the bonfire had been put out at dusk and everyone returned to their huts.

'It's time for me to go,' Vani said to Solly, and they both stood up. The other villagers knew immediately what was going to happen without translation. Willy also stood up and asked Solly to translate one last thing to Vani.

'Next time we see you again, you will be coming from your home country. Please, when you come, bring some brandy for us to enjoy around the fire.' The request left Vani longing for home again, as brandy was the preferred drink around the fire for most Afrikaans South Africans.

Vani replied, 'When I return, I will bring enough brandy to last us two weeks. Thank you again for all your kindness, generosity, and care. Everyone here is a true testament that you don't need much to care for a fellow human being. Thank you, I consider you all my friends and I have been blessed to have met you.'

Solly translated his last words to the villagers and with that, he said his goodbyes with handshakes and hugs and started making his way in the direction of Tete.

Chapter 10

Setting off into the bushveld, Vani felt a sense of nostalgia as he remembered his younger years growing up on the farm. He had spent most of his youth and school holidays on their family farm in the Schoemanskloof area of Mpumalanga province. As a boy he often wandered on his own into the wild, tracking animals, and investigating the nature around him. He developed a keen sense of direction on his childhood adventures which allowed him to wander further each time.

The night sky helped Vani navigate his way through the bushveld; once he had established his direction, he coordinated himself with the stars and kept his course. Walking through the bush at night didn't prove as difficult as anticipated. Vani was astonished by how well he could see at night now. It already felt strange not to wear his glasses, he had depended on them for twenty years. Even the marks around his ears where the glasses had rested had completely disappeared.

Vani moved at a good pace, travelling past the outskirts of the mining site. As he passed the site, he noticed some buildings that looked remarkably familiar. He stood still for a moment to observe them and then he got excited. He recognised the two buildings from a previous work trip when he had been employed by a large company that manufactured explosives for mining applications. The buildings were blast-proof bunkers used for storing mining explosives, detonator cords, detonators, and all the equipment required to conduct large-scale blasting operations on a mining site.

Vani deviated from his course to inspect the security around the buildings. Since the terrorists had moved off the mining site, there were no guards or noticeable security. He walked to one of the poles supporting the high fence to see if he could climb over, and pushed the pole to check its rigidity. And to his surprise the pole moved easily, although it was planted in concrete. Either the pole wasn't planted properly, or his new body came with a lot more strength than he was used to.

Vani managed to push the pole completely over to lie flat on the ground, which meant he could just walk into the compound. He noticed the area was undisturbed, either the terrorists weren't aware of what was inside, or they weren't after the explosives. Getting to the large blast doors he saw that they were only locked with two padlocks. Breaking them open would be easy, he just needed a hard object to hit them with. He reached out and took hold of one padlock and as he pulled experimentally on the bottom part the lock broke open. 'Oh, my freaken word!' Vani said aloud. 'Surely I didn't break the lock, maybe it's a cheap lock from China or something.' Vani took hold of the second padlock and pulled, and he could see now that he had broken the padlocks with his own strength.

Vani opened the blast doors and stepped inside very cautiously, knowing how little static electricity it took to set off a detonator and thus the whole bunker building. From the doorway, he noticed the bunker was fully stocked; he spotted the time delay connectors, the detonator cord, detonators, and packaged mining explosives which were wrapped in plastic casings like large rolls of ham.

'Awesome... just awesome... Whoo-hoo! I'll come back for this for sure,' he muttered with a grin.

Vani made his way out of the compound and back on his course to the town of Tete. As he was walking, he tried to remember how the wiring of a blasting configuration worked. He remembered most of the theory from his training as an explosive engineer. The one item that wasn't in the bunker was the control unit that sets off the detonator cord, which meant he had to start thinking of different ways to ignite the explosives when he found a use for them. It all depended on how he would need to use them – small explosions in close proximity or large explosions from a far distance. He contemplated a few ideas but ended his train of thought with the notion that he'd make a plan when the time came. Without realising it he had come close to the main road, and was reminded how much easier it was to do something tedious when your mind was somewhere else.

Vani started moving parallel to the road while remaining in the bushveld. He saw some movement up ahead in the road where the terrorists had set up a checkpoint. Vani stood still for a while, watching. It looked like they were concentrating on the road so the best approach would be to go wider around them at a slow pace. Just as long as he didn't miss the school which they might be using as a base of operations.

So, Vani first started by crouching and moving forward and as he got closer to the checkpoint he kept lower to the ground. There were a few shrubs and trees which he used as small milestones, moving from one to the other. It took Vani about half an hour to leopard crawl past the checkpoint without being detected. He noticed the terrorists were not very disciplined, they were rowdy and lacked focus.

Once he had cleared the checkpoint and put enough distance between himself and it, Vani went back to moving in a crouching position. He was constantly looking for the school. At last, he spotted the school about a kilometre away and he changed his direction towards the building. As he moved closer, he could see a lot of activity around the school, however, his night vision only allowed him to see the terrorists on his side of the building. Wondering how many there actually were and where they would keep the hostages Vani looked down at the ground and sighed, closing his eyes for an instant.

When he looked up again, without knowing how, his eyesight had changed to thermal imaging, showing him all the heat signatures of the people on the school premises. Vani got such a shock that he stumbled backwards, landing on his behind. He sat in awe, waving his hands in front of his face, seeing his own hands in a thermal spectrum. This freaked Vani out, he started hyperventilating, closed his eyes, and put his head between his knees. He tried to wrap his mind around what was going on, tried to find a reason. After a short while, he managed to calm his breathing, making sure he kept his eyes closed. *This has to be part of the changes that have been happening to me, but how*? Vani thought.

Vani sat for five minutes, concluding that his muscles must not have been the only thing that had changed. The source of the change must have been when he got stabbed because the villagers who helped him saw the changes happen only once he was recovering in the hut. And in his analytical way of thinking the realisation hit him. *That green dagger! It must be that! It was calling to me while it was hanging around that leader's neck. What was that dagger? Why did the blade glow with a green light*?

Vani opened his eyes and his sight had returned to normal. He realised that he truly knew so little of how he had been changed. *And what if the changes aren't complete yet, what else is going to happen to me*? he thought. He moved forward onto his knees, looking at the school, then trying to recreate the thermal imaging. He deliberately thought, *I want to see where everyone is*. But nothing changed in his vision until his instinctive reflexes made him blink his eyes. And there it was again – the heat signatures of everyone in the school.

Looking around slowly he started to understand the depth perception of his new eyesight and thus figure out who was in front of the school and who was behind the school. He also saw two classrooms filled with people sitting on the ground in groups. *That must be them, the hostages*, he thought. *But the groups are so small now, there were a lot more people when we were first captured*. He estimated that about forty people were still being kept hostage.

Testing his new theory, Vani thought, *I want my normal vision*, and he blinked. And just like that, his normal eyesight was restored. 'So, I have to think about it and then blink to change the channel. Interesting and freaken awesome!' he said under his breath. As he moved closer to the school another realisation struck Vani that took his excitement away immediately. This would be the first time he would most likely have to kill someone. He tried to not let the thought of taking another life get to him, however, it kept on looming in the back of his mind. He was not an aggressive person by nature and to do this would be life-altering for him. He reminded himself, *I'm not doing this to revenge myself or anyone, I'm doing this to save my friends and the people in the region.*

Vani snuck closer and closer and started to leopard crawl again once he reached the school. There was a large flowery bush on the premises that he could use as cover. Vani moved through a hole in the school fence and crawled towards the bush where he took cover and made further observations. He tried to identify some pattern or schedule that the terrorists used to patrol the grounds, but there seemed no regularity or reason for their movements, they came and went as they felt like. This made it difficult to make his way to the classrooms. He waited in the bush until eventually the morning sunrise started brightening the sky. The movement had quietened now, and he could see a clear path to the classrooms. Vani crept slowly out from behind the bush and ran to the rear of the school building. Through the windows of the first classroom he saw the hostages, dirty and discouraged, huddled together. Next to them sat four guards in their own group, busy playing a card game. He moved to look through a window of the second classroom. There he saw a similar situation, one large group of hostages and four guards sitting on the ground.

Damn it! he thought. *There is no way of getting in there without some hostages being killed in the process.* Very reluctantly Vani started moving backwards, making his way off the school premises. He moved out of sight and took shelter behind a large tree. *How do I get the hostages out, and if I do manage to get them out, they will make a large and slow-moving group. They would just be shot on sight for trying to escape.*

Damn these assholes for their malice and ruthlessness. I need to come up with a plan. Think Vani. Think!

And then he remembered a book he had read years ago, he remembered as if he had just read it. The book was called *The Art of War* and it had several tactics on war and readiness. 'That's it!' Vani said out loud, only to realise he needed to stay quiet while trying to hide. *That was stupid of me*, he thought. *I must create a diversion. But one big enough to draw all these troops from their position. Something in Tete would be great, something that would also take out a large number of the terrorist group. But, to get them assembled in a specific location in large numbers I guess I would need another type of diversion. But how?*

VANI SPENT THE MORNING pondering different options to get many terrorists assembled. He knew that he had to gather more information on their doings in Tete. Capturing one of the terrorists for information would be pointless, from what he had seen so far that they all spoke Portuguese and no English. So, it would be pointless to try and interrogate one for information. Going into Tete by himself would give him first-hand information and doing it on his own would be easier, as a single person would be harder to spot and he could move around more quickly – though he did not know the town or where to begin. *Well, then I'll just begin at the beginning. I'll go to Tete and move inwards from where I enter the town. I can follow my senses to see where the terrorists are active and then strategise from there. Hmmm... luckily, I have myself to talk to, in situations like this you do want expert advice,* Vani thought and laughed at himself.

IT WAS LATE MORNING when Vani started walking towards Tete. He kept to the cover of the bushveld and the cool shade of the trees. As he got closer to Tete the trees and plant growth became more sparse.

He paused at the last tree on his way in. Between him and Tete there was now about one kilometre of sand and grass patches. No cover at all. The ground was littered with general waste and several abandoned motorcycles lay on the roadside. It would be best to wait in his current location till nightfall and then make his way into the town.

Vani took a seat on the ground and for the first time he started thinking of food as hunger gnawed his stomach. He looked at the area around him, but there was nothing edible. No vegetation like wild fruit, no wildlife, absolutely nothing. He tilted his head back and rested it against the tree, trying to calm himself and get some rest before the night ahead of him. Vani dozed off into a deep sleep in the African heat under the tree with a gentle breeze blowing.

VANI'S NIGHT-TIME ACTIVITIES had taken their toll and when he finally woke up it was already past dusk. Vani got up and looked around. It was quiet. He turned his gaze to the path he would have to take into the town. There was some terrorist movement, however, Vani was confident he could get past them should they still be around when it was dark. And was as he had anticipated, when nightfall came the activity in that part of the town reduced a bit. From time to time, the terrorists drove along the outer road of town, in a convoy of three vehicles. They were driving old pickup trucks, some of which were fitted with heavy machine guns. *Now I know where all the hijacked vehicles go that get stolen in South Africa. The bastards!* Vani thought.

Vani waited till a patrol passed him and then decided to run for a building. He sprinted from his tree, over a small strip of open ground and the first street to an apartment block. The apartment block looked empty, as did most buildings on the outskirts of the town. Making his way through the grounds of the apartment block, he saw no one. The locals who had occupied the apartments must have fled when their town got attacked. *First things first*, Vani thought. He entered the building and went from one apartment to the other in search of food, looking for non-perishables and food that would not give him an upset stomach. He managed to find quite a bit to eat, raw peanuts, cereals, bags of potato chips, canned food, cold drinks, and beer. And in some fridges, there was polony... *'yuck, I fucking hate fucking polony! Bleh!'* he muttered.

He picked one of the top apartments with a view over the town and sat on the balcony to eat while he familiarised himself with the town. He noted a few large buildings as beacon points to help him navigate. And in the centre of the town, there was a sports stadium. After eating some canned corned beef and sardines, he got up to check if the stove was working. He was glad to find it was and using a small pot he boiled seven eggs. The building was quiet, the only sounds were the creaking noises as the building cooled after the heat of the day. It was easy enough to move around at night without getting spotted, but to use his time efficiently he needed to find a way to move around during the day as well. Once his eggs had cooked for eight minutes, Vani peeled off the shells. He sprinkled them lightly with salt and pepper and enjoyed the first decent meal he'd had for days. It was time to go down and survey the town.

Exiting the apartment block, Vani made his way towards the centre of town. He moved quickly from one building to another, aligning his movement with the buildings he had identified earlier. He made substantial progress, crossing five city blocks unnoticed. After the fifth, he spotted groups of terrorists moving through the streets. They were looting businesses and shops. The number of vehicles also increased, which gave Vani the feeling that he was moving in the right direction. Surely if the activity was increasing then their base of operations had to be nearby. Like a hornet's nest, the closer you get, the more hornets you find.

Chapter 11

Vani held his position which was next to another block of apartments, just more run down than the first building he had been in. Another opportunity to get higher and observe more. He made his way slowly up the stairs; there was no sign of anyone but for some reason, he felt uneasy. It was five stories high and would provide a good vantage point to look straight into the middle of the city. He moved to the top floor towards an apartment that would have overlook the direction he wanted.

Vani opened the door softly. And he found a scene he had hoped never to see. On the floor in the living room was a terrorist raping a woman. Her face was bloody from a beating, and she was in tears. She lay in silence, most likely fearing for her life. Frozen and traumatised by what he was seeing, Vani felt his stomach turn. He was confronted with a difficult decision; help her and be a decent human being, or slip away and leave her, ensuring that he remained undiscovered.

However, this was one crime that Vani considered to be crueller than murder, as the victim would have to live with that memory for the rest of their lives. The person would be forever scarred, Vani felt no one could continue a normal life after such an event.

Vani leaped into action. The rapist never saw what was coming. Vani grabbed him from behind by his hair and yanked him up onto his knees, going for a choke hold to try and silently defuse the situation. With one of Vani's arms across his neck and the other squeezing his head from behind, the rapist was choking, his eyes popping out of their sockets, desperately trying to loosen Vani's hold. But it was no use.

The shocked woman scrambled back from the rapist in horror. Vani had choked men before, in his Brazilian jiujutsu classes and in the occasional bar fight, but always maintained control. However, with his new strength Vani underestimated the pressure of his hold. The rapist's windpipe in his throat was crushed and the spine in his neck was broken with a bone-chilling crunch. And then there was just silence.

Vani lay the terrorist down on the floor slowly and looked at the woman. There was a bewildered look in her eyes, she must have thought that she had gone from the frying pan into the fire. Vani stood motionless with the light from the hallway shining behind him only showing his body's outline and to her, he looked larger than life. He extended his hand to help her off the floor, but she was so terrified that she flinched and turned away. Her crying went from silent and withheld to full-out shivering and sobbing. Vani could see she was too frightened to trust him. He moved past her to the door leading to the balcony as she grabbed her dress and ran from the room. He went to close the open door behind her.

From the balcony, Vani could see a lot more of the terrorists' movements. He sat and observed them for the remainder of the night. When daylight broke, he nodded off, waking up at around eleven o'clock. After gathering his thoughts and observing his immediate surroundings, he continued to monitor the terrorist movement. There was a lot of gunfire in the city that morning, though it didn't sound like it was near him or the stadium. Vani started focusing more on the streets and the buildings next to him, trying to figure out a way to move around in the daytime without being seen. And that was when he spotted a manhole cover on the sidewalk. He wondered if the stormwater and sewage pipes were functioning. The last he had heard about Mozambique's wastewater infrastructure was when the current government decided to kick out all the Portuguese settlers many years ago. In anger, the Portuguese people pumped concrete into the wastewater infrastructure to make it unusable for the new government.

Crawling around in the underground concrete pipes wasn't Vani's first choice because he had no idea of how he would navigate himself, and whether the pipes were blocked off and obviously the stench of it all. As he studied their movements from the balcony, it was clear that all vehicles came and went from the sports stadium. Hence the assumption was made that they must've set up their headquarters there. It was now a question of how to get to the sports stadium and see what they were busy with and then plan from there again.

Vani decided to wait till nightfall to cover more ground before exploring the option of going into the sewer pipes. And with that thought he got up to find something to eat and drink. The body on the floor was starting to attract flies. Vani dragged the corpse – neck crushed and still pants-less – to a bedroom and closed the door behind it, wondering why he hadn't checked the building last night with his thermal vision before entering the room. He felt frustrated for forgetting about his new abilities, knowing he could've handled the situation differently.

Vani continued to the kitchen for food. To his surprise, there was fruit in the fridge as well as beer and salted dried fish. He sat down in the living room to enjoy his lunch. 'I wonder how long a person can talk to themselves before it becomes a permanent mental problem?' Vani said. 'These are challenging times and cruel circumstances; I wouldn't want anyone else here anyway, so I guess it is kind of for the best.'

After finishing his lunch, he used his thermal vision to check the building for any signs of life. Finding that he was again alone in the building, he positioned himself in a seated position to have another nap while he waited for the night.

When night came, Vani was well rested and had eaten enough. It was time to move. He left the apartment and went down the dark stairwell, which to him seemed perfectly lit. Coming out of the building he saw patrols driving a few streets away. There were six city blocks between Vani and the sports stadium. After making his way through three blocks the level of terrorist movement increased significantly. There were a lot of foot soldiers coming and going from the sports stadium, it seemed they were coming from the battle lines to resupply from the stadium and then headed out to fight again. Vani managed to cross one more city block and took refuge in a tyre retail shop which had already been ransacked. There was a lot of open floor space inside the building, and on the same premises, there was a manhole cover that connected with the sewage pipe network. From this point forward he thought it would be best to move through the sewer pipes.

Vani managed to lift the concrete manhole cover with only his hands, wondering what the limit of his new strength was. *Well, let me get through this whole experience, I'll figure out what changes have been going on and what my limits are once I get home. Because I am going home*, he thought. He also made a mental note to remember to get every injection possible for the treatment of hepatitis A to Z once he was back.

Crawling through the sewers was as bad as he'd expected; awful, smelly, slimy, and wet. He navigated well making use of the stormwater inlet holes, and before long, he was on the sports stadium premises. He moved around the stadium in the underground pipe network, slightly lifting and peeking through every manhole cover he found. He finally found a cover that was completely in the dark, below the concrete seats and next to supporting pillars with no people around it. Vani clambered out and prepared to do his surveying of their operations. He used the steel anchor bolts on a pillar to climb high for a bird's eye view. Every sinew and muscle fibre strained and bulged as he ascended to a dizzying height and he whispered to himself, 'Look at me Mom, I'm a real ninja now.' Vani finally reached the highest point where it joined and supported an I beam for the roof structure. He settled down to assess the scene below.

The terrorists had made the stadium their home and storage point. It was separated into different operations. The viewing boxes had been turned into sleeping quarters, probably for their senior soldiers. The foot soldiers had made their own shack-like structures on the stadium's concrete chairs. The commentary box, with the best view of the whole stadium, was occupied by Koji Bemin. Vani could clearly see him gazing out of the window at the movements of his army below.

Roughly judging it looked like there were five to seven thousand people in the stadium. About three-quarters of the sports field had been kept open with a podium at the closed end, used for addressing the soldiers and preaching propaganda. The other part of the sports field was stacked high with several types of munitions.

Vani inched carefully into the roof structure and made his way over to the commentary box. He used the steel roof structure like a giant jungle-gym for adults and made his way from truss to truss. It was a far way down should he fall, so he moved slowly and carefully, always ensuring he had more than one point of contact. The bright floodlights shining down onto the stadium hid Vani from prying eyes, blinding the terrorists on the ground to his movement behind the lights.

He eventually got close to Koji, who was oblivious to Vani's presence. Looking at him, Vani could feel his blood stirring with rage, resisting the urge to take action at that moment. Then Vani noticed the dagger around his neck, Koji's most prized possession. Vani sat perched like a bird for a while longer, locking onto the dagger. *That's it*! he thought. *I've found my first distraction to build up to the second distraction!*

Vani started planning the logistics around his grand scheme. *If I were to steal that dagger from Koji, he would be so infuriated that he would assemble all his troops and give them the order to hunt me down. That is when I need to strike hard, when he is assembling them. So,*

I would need to have my secondary plan in place before starting with the first. As the plan began to crystalise in Vani's mind, he retreated through the roof structure and made his way back through the sewers to the abandoned tyre shop.

Chapter 12

It was approaching 3 am. Vani sat on a crate in the tyre shop, figuring out what to do next. That's when he had a light bulb moment. 'Ah, yes,' he said, 'of course!' and then paused while he thought some more. He had a plan; however, it was scattered puzzle pieces, he needed to get the sequence of events right to make the picture complete. Moving his fingers around in the air and mumbling to himself he finally got to the clear mental picture he wanted. His eyes lit up as he scribbled the points onto a sheet of paper.

Step 1: Head out of town and back to the mining site's explosive bunkers. On the way back collect whatever luggage bags and rope I can find in the apartment blocks. Move as fast as possible to make the most of the little night-time that was left. Push my body and new abilities to see if this long distance could be covered in such a short time.

Step 2: At the bunker, carefully pack the explosives into the bags. Using the wire fence outside, construct a type of cargo net that I can fit all the bags into so that I have only one large item to carry on my back. All the explosive components would probably weigh over 2500 kilograms in total. Depending on how much I can carry with my new strength, the limit might be on the fence used as a cargo net. If so, it will mean making multiple trips over multiple days.

Step 3: Getting back into town may be a challenge, I'll have to cross all the city blocks in one night and get the explosives into the tyre shop. Previously it took me two nights to cover the distance without carrying any extra weight. Though it's not necessary to complete the section through the bushveld in one night, it's essential to move through town in one night. Utilise my new sense of sight a lot more.

Step 4: In the tyre shop, unpack the explosives and group the items together. Once sorted, put components together that work with each other. Create explosive packages which could be assembled on site without making unnecessary trips through the sewer.

Step 5: Manoeuvre through the sewer and storm water pipe maze under the sports stadium planting explosive packages at key supporting points to ensure maximum effect. Force some into the rain drainage system directly under the sports field, as the field is the main target. Connect explosive wires correctly and into a single wire and run it all the way back to the tyre shop for detonation. Will need a spark or fire to set it off.

Step 6: After all the explosives are planted, wait for night-time when Koji is asleep. Enter via the sewers and move across the stadium in the roof structure. From there, drop down to the commentary box. To ensure Koji's full rage, leave a note with the lyrics that I sang when Koji plunged the dagger into my chest. Steal the dagger!

Step 7: Observe the sports stadium constantly. If I'm right, there'll be an influx of soldiers returning to the stadium the next morning. Listen carefully to the announcement system of the stadium. Once I hear the ramblings of the lunatic, it's time to ignite the charge. After the explosion, make my way back to the school to free the hostages.

THE ACTUAL EVENTS CLOSELY mirrored Vani's plan except for a few surprises. Because of Vani's new body, he managed to get back to the mine's bunkers that same night. The following night he completed four trips between the town and the bunkers, the wire strength of the fence was the limiting factor as to how much weight he could carry. His strength left him in disbelief, but he started to understand a bit more about the new Vani. The explosives were planted all around and underneath the stadium. But stealing the dagger proved more challenging than he had anticipated...

To get off the roof structure and onto the stadium seats, Vani had to move to the back end of the stadium where the high seats were closest to the roof. He managed to get down by manoeuvring onto a concrete pillar, however, Vani knew climbing back up the pillar would be difficult due to the smooth surface. He turned his attention to the task at hand and started crawling downwards towards the commentary box, using the seats as cover. As he got close to the commentary box's door, he spotted two guards which he had not seen from his vantage point in the roof structure.

Staring at the guards between the stadium seats, Vani started thinking. *Taking them out is one thing, taking them out without drawing attention to me is another thing altogether. Plus, I'm sure that they aren't the standard run-of-the-mill soldiers, they must be pretty tough if they're overseeing their leader's security.* The bright stadium lights didn't work in Vani's favour any longer and more consideration was required. Vani spent such a long time contemplating his options that he was surprised to see the one guard stepping away from his position and going around the corner to urinate. *YES, this is my chance*! thought Vani. He crawled behind the chairs in the direction of the guard that had gone to relieve himself.

Vani moved stealthily until he was close to the guard and stood up slowly behind the man. He used his speed and strength to leap forward, covering the guard's mouth with one hand and grasping his neck with the other, instantly crushing his throat and breaking his neck. He gently laid the dead guard down on the ground. Knowing that the other guard would expect his comrade to come back, Vani took advantage of this. He walked casually around the corner to the door where the remaining guard was standing. The guard assumed it was his comrade returning and didn't look in Vani's direction until it was too late. Vani grabbed him from behind and crushed his neck. For a second Vani wished he had a more creative way of doing this, however, the method he used for killing terrorists was working and that was all that mattered at that moment.

With both guards down, Vani opened the door cautiously and stepped inside. There he was, Koji Bemin sleeping, at his most vulnerable. Vani stood by the door watching Koji, he could feel his heart pounding harder and harder. Rage was consuming Vani. He heard the blood flowing in his ears, his breathing became shallower. Vani closed his eyes and started the breathing exercise, which he had used in the past when sparring in his martial arts training to calm his mind. The controlled breathing helped to compose him and stopped his racing thoughts of taking action to indulge his desire for revenge.

Feeling calmer, Vani opened his eyes and scanned the room for the dagger. He spotted it on a table next to some of Koji's personal belongings. He moved quietly over to the table and slowly picked it up. It felt heavier than he had anticipated, and the blood had been cleaned off it. From his pants pocket, he took out the note with the lyrics he had sung when he was stabbed and placed the paper on the side table where the dagger had been.

Vani retreated slowly and closed the door behind him. He took a deep breath and sighed, releasing some of the tension. *Hope this plan works and I didn't make a mistake by letting him live. I'll find out tomorrow*, he thought. Looking around he didn't spot any new movement close by, he got back down to a crawling position and made his way to the top of the stairs. Approaching the concrete pillar, he wondered whether he should try jumping and grabbing the sides of the pillar to scale it, although it was five metres from where the concrete pillar met the steel roof structure.

Vani squatted next to the pillar in preparation for his jump. He shot his body upwards and to his shock, his strong legs launched him so high he was in between the steel tubes and I beams of the roof structure. He desperately grabbed onto a pole next to him, his heart was racing again. 'Seriously, what is going on with me? How is this possible?' he said under his breath. He found a safer footing on the roof structure, composed himself and started making his way out of the stadium.

VANI CLIMBED OUT OF the sewer at around 4:30 am and laid the last bit of the detonation cord into the tyre shop from where he would ignite it. Vani was dirty, hungry, and exhausted, and as he sat waiting for all hell to break loose, he started thinking of what a normal day would've been for him. At 06:15 am gunshots started going off from the stadium which snapped him out of his daydream, as he remembered the big task at hand. At 06:30 many pickup trucks made their way to the stadium, filled with soldiers from the front lines. The gunshots increased as the terrorists fired their weapons into the air to stir their blood. Then Vani heard the raging rambling of a madman over the announcement system, he knew it was time to end it.

Vani held the cord to ignite it and the realisation hit him. *How the fuck did I not bring something to light it with?! Fucking stupid Vani! Fuck!* Vani was overcome with rage at his own mistake. In that moment of desperation, Vani discovered a new ability. His muscles were starting to glow green, his spine was expanding, and the stored energy from the Nagapie's power source was building up, getting ready to be released. There came a gush of wind into the tyre shop which whirled around Vani, encircling him. Vani felt a power coming from within, it felt strong, it felt warm, it felt right. He stretched the hand that held the detonation cord out in front of him and focused his energy on it. A massive jolt of energy was released from Vani's hand, it blew a huge hole in the wall in front of him, disintegrated the bricks, and thankfully, also ignited the cord.

The stormy conditions around Vani calmed immediately as he heard the first of many explosions. It was a lot louder than he had expected. Vani stared towards the stadium, wishing he had some awesome background music for this momentous occasion. The timing of the explosives was near-perfect, following each other in split-second intervals, creating the desired effect of the entire sports stadium collapsing on itself and the sports field swallowing everyone and everything on it.

Vani watched in awe as a large dust cloud was blown out in a circular motion from the stadium. It darkened the sky, eclipsing the sun over the stadium and three city blocks around it. A deadly silence settled over the town.

Vani turned away from the stadium, attaching the stolen dagger on his belt. He needed to move quickly now to take advantage of the confusion. He started running towards the school, moving as fast as he could. Not a soul in sight in the town. Running through the bushveld, the blades of grass blurred past Vani, as he reached a speed of eighty kilometres per hour.

At the school the soldiers were indeed in a panic. Shouting, running around loading supplies and getting ready to retreat. Without hesitation, he ran onto the school grounds making his way to the classrooms where the hostages were kept. To his shock the classrooms were empty. A soldier came around the corner and Vani grabbed him, knocking the rifle out of his hands and lifting the soldier up by his neck. Vani pointed into the classroom and asked frantically, 'Where are they? What did you do with the people?' The soldier, struggling to breathe, pointed in the direction of the road towards Moatize.

Vani activated his thermal vision, and there they were, the group of hostages running away from the terrorist's threat. Vani felt relieved and for some reason, he also felt vindicated. They were free. The plan worked and the terrorists let the hostages go. He had managed to save them. Vani dropped the soldier to follow the hostages. The soldier scrambled on the ground to pick up his rifle as Vani was walking away, aimed, and pulled the trigger.

The shot went off and hit Vani in the back. He felt the impact of the bullet and immediately assumed the worst. It was so loud that it drowned out all other sounds and left only a ringing noise in Vani's ears. He whirled around in disbelief as the enraged soldier fired off three more shots towards Vani. Shocked, he looked down at his torso, tried to feel where the holes were, tried to see the blood. Something didn't feel right. From what Vani had heard, being shot was an extremely painful burning sensation.

But there was nothing, no holes, no blood, and no pain. Vani's enhanced skin had prevented the bullets from penetrating his body. The soldier's eyes widened in fear as Vani's focus fell on him, and he leaped forward, again grabbing the soldier by the neck. Vani lifted him, looked him in the eyes, and snapped his neck like it was a toothpick. He dropped the lifeless body and ran after the hostages. He caught up with them quickly, waving and shouting to get their attention.

Jacob saw it was Vani calling to them and he immediately ran to his friend where they embraced each other in a long brotherly hug. 'I thought you were dead, my boy!' said Jacob, with tears in his eyes. 'I'm so glad and grateful to see you're still alive!'

Vani replied, also filled with emotion, 'You should know better; I couldn't leave you here to have all the fun. Where is Benjamin? I can't see him. Surely, he would've made it with his charisma?'

'Sorry my boy, they killed Benjamin three nights ago. One of our captors was going to rape a hostage, and Benjamin tried to defend her. They shot him in cold blood in front of us all,' Jacob said, despondently.

Chapter 13

'Do you know where we should go?' Jacob asked. The entire group of rescued hostages looked at Vani. 'Yes, I think I do. We should go back towards Tete and make for the airport. There was still some gunfighting there before the explosion. I assume that there's a military presence that has prevented the terrorists from taking over the airport,' Vani replied.

'What was that huge explosion? We felt the earth shake in the classrooms and when we got released there was a massive mushroom-like cloud over Tete. Did someone drop a nuke on the terrorists?' Jacob asked.

Vani looked down at his dirty attire and broken shoes still laced with sewage. 'No, there was no nuke... just normal explosives in a high dosage.' He turned to the group. 'You should follow me; we will be travelling in the bushveld behind the school and make our way to Tete. I have used the path a few times recently. The road might be quicker, but I don't want to risk losing anyone in unnecessary conflict with the remainder of the enemy's forces.'

'Can I get a gun from the school, Vani?' Jacob asked. 'I want to kill some of these fuckers for what they have done!'

Vani shook his head. 'let's not waste time. I think a straight line to the airport might get us out of this mess before nightfall.'

'Then you lead the way and get us out of here, no detours,' Jacob conceded.

The group fell into a single line and walked behind Vani as he made his way into the bushveld. Vani used his thermal vision as they walked to ensure there was no threat. About a kilometre into their journey, he noticed a person's thermal signature between some long grass under the shade of a tree. The person was lying completely still. Their path would go straight past the person in hiding.

Vani kept their direction and moved at a slow pace for everyone to stick together. Getting closer to the mystery person it became clear he was not a terrorist. It was a fully camouflaged soldier from someone's army. About twenty metres from the soldier in hiding, Vani told the group to hold their position while he scouted ahead. Vani kept his course and walked up right next to the soldier. Looking up at the sky as if he was assessing the weather, Vani spoke quietly. 'No one from our group can see you. Please don't attack them. We were all hostages captured by the terrorists and we are making our way to the airport at Tete. I just need to know, are we moving in the right direction, and will there be help for us there? If the answer is yes to both those questions, please make two clicking sounds with your tongue.'

'Tsk tsk,' came back from the tall grass.

'Thank you,' Vani responded still looking at the sky. He called the group to start moving again and they carried on with their journey. None of them noticed the incognito soldier who was in fact a member of the Recce unit from South Africa – a specialised unit used for reconnaissance deep in enemy territory. The soldier held his position, silently observing the group passing by, before messaging his commanding officer with the news of the survivors and their planned destination.

Getting closer to Tete, Vani could see that there was increased movement around the town since the explosion. Though it didn't look like terrorists, perhaps some locals trying to get back their homes. The group marched along the outskirts of town but eventually they had to enter the town to cross the bridge spanning the wide and majestic Zambezi River. The bridge led into the part of town where the airport was situated.

The town looked like a war zone, with buildings in ruins and corpses buzzing with flies. The freed hostages looked on in horror, all of them foreign nationals, and none were aware of the destruction that a terrorist group could wreak.

Approaching the bridge, Vani spotted locals running towards the destroyed stadium. They were no doubt, going to see what had happened and to claim whatever was left for them. At the entrance to the bridge was a military control point, poorly protected by sandbags which were riddled with bullet holes. The military personnel weren't friendly and understandably so, they had been engaged in gunfights for more than two weeks. However, as soon as the military personnel spotted the foreigners, they moved swiftly towards the group to escort them over the bridge into the safe zone. The army had been told about the foreign hostages, though they were not aware of their condition and their whereabouts.

Once over the bridge, the group was loaded onto a truck and driven to a military base where they were given medical attention. Vani didn't want anyone to know of the changes he had been going through and knew the medical examination might reveal his new secret. So, while undergoing his examination he told the doctor that his religion did not allow him to stick anything into his body and if they wanted to give him medication, it would have to be orally, not knowing if such a thing even existed. All he knew was that no needle was going to be strong enough to pierce his skin seeing as a bullet from an AK47 couldn't make a scratch. While Vani was explaining to the doctor that he was fine, a man walked into the medical tent.

The man had an authoritative air about him, he appeared confident and unfazed by the surroundings. He strode past the rescued hostages, glancing at their injuries, and then made his way over to Vani. 'I need you to come with me,' the man said, with an American accent.

Vani nodded and got up to follow the man. They left the medical tent and walked across the military base into a brick building. Inside, a team of people worked busily on computers, scrolling through photos of the terrorists and pages of info. In the centre of the room was a large TV screen with a satellite image of the sports stadium in ruins.

Vani kept following the American to the middle of the room when he suddenly stopped and finally introduced himself. 'I'm Agent Smith, and I'm from the CIA. It is genuinely nice to finally meet you.' Vani got a chill running down his spine, immediately assuming the worst. Agent Smith continued. 'We've been tracking this terrorist cell for months, especially their leader, Koji Bemin. Do you know of him?'

Vani took a deep breath to keep calm and responded, 'I've had the misfortune of meeting him in the last few weeks, so yes, I do know of him.' He didn't want to say anything more than what was asked. The agent kept silent, trying to get Vani to elaborate, but Vani just kept quiet, staring at the agent.

'You know, we couldn't believe that a civilian could cause this type of damage,' the agent said, pointing at the TV screen. 'Well, at least not until we put your profile together. You have been unknowingly trained your whole life for this event. The career choices you made, the fitness activities you did. Every choice you ever made led up to this spectacular display of human perseverance.' The agent moved to a desk to pick up a file with Vani's name on it. 'You are one interesting person. If you were ten years younger, I would offer you a job right now. Of course, I would first get you to shower and clean up, hehe,' he said, laughing. 'There are some anomalies, which perhaps you can explain. We've had some technical issues with our satellite connection from this location. Some of the timing seems strange. We could only pick you up once, and that was when you got back out of the sewers and went into this tyre retail building. That's how we know it was you that killed nearly seven thousand terrorists in one blow.'

Agent Smith again paused to build up the silence, to try and get a reaction out of Vani. 'Not a man of many words, I see. You don't have anything to fear. In fact, you are here for a big thank you and a fat pay cheque. We have nothing but admiration for what you did, you managed to do what an entire army could not do.' Vani's eyebrow lifted and he asked, 'Pay cheque?' Agent Smith got a grin on his face 'Yes, Koji Bemin has been on our Most Wanted list for several years, we set up this operation in an attempt to capture him, dead or alive. And now, thanks to you, his remains are splattered all over that stadium debris and rubble. And thus, the reward is yours. It's a once-off payment, there are no strings attached.'

Vani, now a bit more relaxed, asked, 'How much is the bounty on his head? And is there perhaps a chance of getting permanent residency in the USA with this reward?'

'The reward for Koji was ten million US dollars. However, my good man, because of your actions our stay in this shit hole has been dramatically reduced from months to a few weeks. And for that I have the authority to also arrange for citizenship for you and your two daughters, Astrid and Kate. I assume you don't want your Ex coming with you. Hehe! The US embassy in South Africa will contact you shortly to collect your permanent residency cards.'

Overrun with emotion and gratitude, Vani shook Agent Smith's hand 'Thank you! For this meeting and everything.' Vani let go of his hand to wipe a tear running down his face. 'I can't wait to see my daughters.'

'Oh yes,' Agent Smith said, 'you also get a ride home right now in our helicopter. The other rescued hostages will follow you shortly.'

'If it's fine with you, I would like to wait for Jacob, my colleague. I risked a lot to get him out. I would very much like to see him go home,' Vani requested.

'Of course, your helicopter will leave tomorrow morning then with you two gentlemen onboard,' Agent Smith said. 'Now let me show you to the ablution block.'

'Oh, one last request, please, Vani asked, suddenly considering the safety of his children and possible revenge attacks on him. 'Can you keep my name out of the press and media? I don't want anyone else to know what role I played here.'

'You were a hostage in this saga, nothing else. The stadium blew up because of improper storage of highly explosive munitions,' Agent Smith said, with a wink.

Chapter 14

Vani entered the ablution block with soap and clothing from the CIA. He stood in front of a mirror, realising he hadn't seen his own face for about a month. He studied his reflection up and down. Looking at the clothing he was still wearing, he remembered Solly and their kindness. The clothes were now torn, dirty, and smelly. *The people in that CIA office must have smelled me from a mile away*, he thought. Stripping off the filthy clothes, he dropped them on the floor, still looking into the mirror, turning his head to see his body from all angles. He was stunned. He had developed the muscle definition of a world-class athlete. Before this trip, his build was average at best, perhaps carrying a few kilograms. He slowly swung his arms in large circles and stretched them out. Vani grinned. He liked his new body.

The shower lasted for twenty minutes. Vani washed his entire body three times to ensure he'd got all the grime off. Leaving the ablution block dressed in fresh clothes and flip-flops he saw some of the rescued hostages coming out of the medical tent. He went to see if he could spot Jacob. Jacob was nearly done with his medical examination, so Vani went and sat next to him on the bed. Jacob looked him up and down and smiled. 'I never knew you had hair, I always assumed you shaved it short because you were bald. And... hmmm... you smell as sweet as a flower now.' Vani and Jacob burst into laughter.

That night the rescued hostages slept in a large canvas army tent on army bunk beds. And in comparison to the last couple of weeks, everyone agreed it felt like a five-star hotel.

THE NEXT MORNING VARIOUS vehicles moved around the military compound, mostly from different governments coming to collect their citizens. The rescued hostages were escorted to a reception area where their respective governments collected them, everyone except Vani and Jacob. They were taken to an undisclosed site where a black helicopter awaited them. They were the only passengers on board. The helicopter took off in a southwestern direction, flying over the border into South Africa.

Jacob's address was plotted into the GPS and the two-hour flight passed silently as Jacob and Vani stared out down at the landscape below, each deep in thought.

The pilot announced that they were approaching Jacob's house and as the helicopter descended lower and lower towards the tricky landing spot, Jacob's family came out to see what the noise was about. The helicopter touched down in the street in front of his house, and when Jacob got out, his wife fell to her knees with a gasp, believing she was witnessing a miracle. She burst into tears as Jacob ran into her arms. Jacob held his family tight as the helicopter took off again.

'I have an easier landing spot in mind for you,' Vani said to the pilot.

'Oh yeah, and where might that be?' the pilot asked. Vani gave him the address and they were on their way.

Flying over Johannesburg into Pretoria, Vani felt a familiar sense of home. As the pilot approached the landing coordinates, he saw it was a school. 'Wow, you did pick a much nicer landing spot, thanks buddy!' the pilot remarked. The drop-off point was Vani's girls' school. He guided the pilot towards the sports field for the landing. Flying over the school buildings they saw there was a sports day taking place at the school. This was the interschool athletics day. Kids were cheering the athletes from the pavilion with songs and the sports ground was full of activity. There was a podium for the winners in the middle of the field in the centre of the pavilion.

The pilot circled three times over the sports field to find a spot that had no children close to it. The singing and athletes all come to a stop as the whole school looked on in awe and excitement, thinking that the helicopter event was pre-organised. The helicopter touched down lightly and Vani thanked the pilot and got out. He walked over the field making his way to the teachers' stand next to the podium noticing the curious whispers as everyone wondered who he was.

At the teacher's podium Vani spotted the principal and called her aside. He introduced himself and explained that he was eager to be reunited with his daughters. The principal asked Vani to accompany her to the podium and making use of the announcement system she called out the following: 'Astrid and Kate from Grade 3, please come to the podium. There is someone special here to see you.'

The girls made their way through the crowd on the pavilion still with no idea who was standing there waiting for them. When they got halfway to the podium, Astrid looked up at the adults and recognised her father. With the loudest scream that entire day and in uncontrollable joy she shouted and ran to her father. 'Pappa! Pappa! Pappa!' When Kate realised that Astrid was right, she also ran as fast as she could to her father with the entire school cheering them on. The girls almost tackled Vani off his feet as all three held each other tightly, like they weren't planning on ever letting go.

'Mommy and the people on the TV said you were dead,' sobbed Astrid. 'But I didn't believe them!'

'Where were you?' Kate asked. 'Did you run away from the bad people?'

Vani wiped their tears of joy and caressed their faces. 'I'll tell you all about it. But for now, let's just be happy to be together.' The principal stepped back to the microphone to enlighten the watching crowd of teachers, children and parents.

'This is Kate and Astrid's father. He was caught in the terrorist attack in Mozambique, and he was presumed dead. What a miracle to see them reunited! Everyone, clap your hands for Kate and Astrid's father!' The whole school went insane with excitement and joy, cheering and applauding. It was indeed a special occasion. Everyone shared in the relief and happiness.

ZOOMING OUT OF THEIR galaxy, on the planet Helderwoud, one of AnaTi's enslaved scientists – a peculiar creature with four arms and six eyes – detected an energy spike from a distant galaxy on his radar system. When he noticed it, he got cold shivers and sweat started dripping from his head. He recognised the energy signature. And at that moment the chief warrior serving AnaTi noticed the scientist's reaction and asked him what was going on. The scientist didn't want to reveal what he'd seen but fearing for his life, he told the warrior that he had detected an energy signature similar to that which the Nagapie had created. The Nagapie had been wiped out many years earlier, so there was no one to recreate their energy source.

The warrior ran to tell AnaTi and when they got back to the scientist workstation, the scientist showed AnaTi the readings on the radar. AnaTi kept quiet, but his fangs started to show as he got excited for the first time in centuries. He turned to the warrior, Juju, with the instructions: 'Give the order for the armada to prepare for long-distance interstellar travel. Assemble the warriors' guild, we have preparations to do. I want what is owed to me.'

The energy spike was from the day that Vani had been stabbed with the green dagger and the enhanced DNA with the Nagapie's power source was released. Now a threat never experienced by humanity was coming straight for them. Their saviour was unaware of the threat, and he had little time to figure out what his new abilities were, where they came from, and how to use them.

To be continued...

About the Author

Victor Frederijk was born in Pretoria, South Africa in 1982. He is a Mechanical Engineer with a passion for storytelling. He enjoys writing novels where the boundaries between gritty fiction and science fiction overlap, creating more realistic characters. His debut book the Dagger of Destiny is the first in a series of works.